ISAAC ASIMOV'S ROBOT CITY™

ALSO AVAILABLE

Published by ibooks, inc.:

ISAAC ASIMOV'S ROBOT CITY

BOOK 2: SUSPICION
MIKE MCQUAY

ibooks
new york
www.ibooks.net

DISTRIBUTED BY SIMON & SCHUSTER, INC.

A Publication of ibooks, inc.

An ibooks, inc. Book

Distributed by Simon & Schuster, Inc.
1230 Avenue of the Americas, New York, NY 10020

ibooks, inc.
24 West 25th Street
New York, NY 10010

The ibooks World Wide Web Site Address is:
http://www.ibooks.net

ISBN 0-7434-7911-4
First ibooks, inc. printing June 2004
10 9 8 7 6 5 4 3 2 1

Edited by David M. Harris

Printed in the U.S.A.

For Brian Shelton and the "bruised banana"

CONTENTS

THE LAWS OF HUMANICS
ISAAC ASIMOV

I am pleased by the way in which the Robot City books pick up the various themes and references in my robot stories and carry on with them.

For instance, my first three robot novels were, essentially, murder mysteries, with Elijah Baley as the detective. Of these first three, the second novel, *The Naked Sun,* was a locked-room mystery, in the sense that the murdered person was found with no weapon on the site and yet no weapon could have been removed either.

I managed to produce a satisfactory solution but I did not do that sort of thing again, and I am delighted that Mike McQuay has tried his hand at it here.

The fourth robot novel, *Robots and Empire,* was not primarily a murder mystery. Elijah Baley had died a natural death at a good, old age, the book veered toward the Foundation universe so that it was clear that both my notable series, the Robot series and the Foundation series, were going to be fused into a broader whole. (No, I didn't do this for some arbitrary reason. The necessities arising out of writing sequels in the 1980s to tales originally written in the 1940s and 1950s forced my hand.)

In *Robots and Empire,* my robot character, Giskard, of whom I was very fond, began to concern himself with "the Laws of Humanics," which, I indicated, might eventually serve as the basis for the science of psychohistory, which plays such a large role in the Foundation series.

Strictly speaking, the Laws of Humanics should be a description, in concise form, of how human beings actually behave. No such description exists, of course. Even psychologists, who study the matter scientifically (at least, I hope they do) cannot present any "laws" but can only make lengthy and diffuse descriptions of what people seem to do. And none of them are prescriptive. When a psychologist says that people respond in this way to a stimulus of that sort, he merely means that some do at some times. Others may do it at other times, or may not do it at all.

If we have to wait for actual laws prescribing human behavior in order to establish psychohistory (and surely we must) then I suppose we will have to wait a long time.

Well, then, what are we going to do about the Laws of Humanics? I suppose what we can do is to start in a very small way, and then later slowly build it up, if we can.

Thus, in *Robots and Empire*, it is a robot, Giskard, who raises the question of the Laws of Humanics. Being a robot, he must view everything from the standpoint of the Three Laws of Robotics—these robotic laws being truly prescriptive, since robots are forced to obey them and cannot disobey them.

The Three Laws of Robotics are:

1—A robot may not injure a human being, or, through inaction, allow a human being to come to harm.

2—A robot must obey the orders given it by human beings except where such orders would conflict with the First Law.

3—A robot must protect its own existence as long as such protection does not conflict with the First or Second Law.

Well, then, it seems to me that a robot could not help but think that human beings ought to behave in such a way as to make it easier for robots to obey those laws.

In fact, it seems to me that ethical human beings should be as anxious to make life easier for robots as the robots themselves would. I took up this matter in my story "The Bicentennial Man," which was published in 1976. In it, I had a human character say in part:

"If a man has the right to give a robot any order that does not involve harm to a human being, he should have the decency never to give a robot any order that involves harm to a robot, unless human safety absolutely requires it. With great power goes great responsibility, and if the robots have Three Laws to protect men, is it too much to ask that men have a law or two to protect robots?"

For instance, the First Law is in two parts. The first part, "A robot may not injure a human being," is absolute and nothing need be done about that. The second part, "or, through inaction, allow a human being to come to harm," leaves things open a bit. A human being might be about to come to harm because of some event involving an inanimate object. A heavy weight might be likely to fall upon him, or he may slip and be about to fall into a lake, or any one of uncountable other misadventures of the sort may be involved. Here the robot simply must try to rescue the human being; pull him from under, steady him on his feet and so on. Or a human being might be threatened by some form of life other than human—a lion, for instance—and the robot must come to his defense.

But what if harm to a human being is threatened by the action of another human being? There a robot must decide what to do. Can he save one human being without harming the other? Or if there must be harm, what course of action must he pursue to make it minimal?

It would be a lot easier for the robot, if human beings were as concerned about the welfare of human beings, as robots are expected to be. And, indeed, any reasonable human code of ethics would instruct human beings to care for each other and to do no harm to each other. Which is, after all, the mandate that humans gave robots. Therefore the First Law of Humanics from the robots' standpoint is:

1—A human being may not injure another human being, or, through inaction, allow a human being to come to harm.

If this law is carried through, the robot will be left guarding the human being from misadventures with inanimate objects and with non-human life, something which poses no ethical dilemmas for it. Of course, the robot must still guard against harm done a human being *unwittingly* by another human being. It must also stand ready to come to the aid of a threatened human being, if another human being on the scene simply cannot get to the scene of action quickly enough. But then, even a robot may *unwittingly* harm a human being, and even a robot may not be fast enough to get to the scene of action in time or skilled enough to take the necessary action. Nothing is perfect.

That brings us to the Second Law of Robotics, which compels a robot to obey all orders given it by human beings except where such orders would conflict with the First Law. This means that human beings can give robots any order without limitation as long as it does not involve harm to a human being.

But then a human being might order a robot to do something impossible, or give it an order that might involve a robot in a dilemma that would do damage to its brain. Thus, in my short story "Liar!," published in 1940, I had a human being deliberately put a robot into a dilemma where its brain burnt out and ceased to function.

We might even imagine that as a robot becomes more intelligent and self-aware, its brain might become sensitive enough to undergo harm if it were forced to do something needlessly embarrassing or undignified. Consequently, the Second Law of Humanics would be:

2—*A human being must give orders to a robot that preserve robotic existence, unless such orders cause harm or discomfort to human beings*.

The Third Law of Robotics is designed to protect the robot, but from the robotic view it can be seen that it does not go far enough. The robot must sacrifice its existence if the First or Second Law makes that necessary. Where the First Law is concerned, there can be no argument. A robot must give up its existence if that is the only way it can avoid doing harm to a human being or can prevent harm from coming to a human being. If we admit the innate superiority of any human being to any robot (which is something I am a little reluctant to admit, actually), then this is inevitable.

On the other hand, must a robot give up its existence merely in obedience to an order that might be trivial, or even malicious? In "The Bicentennial Man," I have some hoodlums deliberately order a robot to take itself apart for the fun of watching that happen. The Third Law of Humanics must therefore be:

3—A human being must not harm a robot, or, through inaction, allow a robot to come to harm, unless such harm is needed to keep a human being from harm or to allow a vital order to be carried out.

Of course, we cannot enforce these laws as we can the Robotic Laws. We cannot design human brains as we design robot brains. It is, however, a beginning, and I honestly think that if we are to have power over intelligent robots, we must feel a corresponding responsibility for them, as the human character in my story "The Bicentennial Man" said.

Certainly in Robot City, these are the sorts of rules that robots might suggest for the only human beings on the planet, as you may soon learn.

It was sunset in the city of robots, and it was snowing paper.

The sun was a yellow one and the atmosphere, mostly nitrogen/oxygen blue, was flush with the veins of iron oxides that traced through it, making the whole twilight sky glow bright orange like a forest fire.

The one who called himself Derec marveled at the sunset from the back of the huge earthmover as it slowly made its way through the city streets, crowds of robots lining the avenue to watch him and his companions make this tour of the city. The tiny shards of paper floated down from the upper stories of the crystal-like buildings, thrown (for reasons that escaped Derec) by the robots that crowded the windows to watch him.

Derec took it all in, sure that it must have significance or the robots wouldn't do it. And that was the only thing he was sure of—for Derec was a person without memory, without notion of who he was. Worse still, he had come to this impossible world, unpopulated by humans, by means that still astounded him; and he had no idea, *no idea,* of where in the universe he was.

He was young, the cape of manhood still new on his shoulders, and he only knew that by observing himself in a mirror. Even his name—Derec—wasn't really his. It was a borrowed name, a convenient thing to call himself because not having a name was like not existing. And he desperately wanted to exist, to know who, to know *what* he was.

And why.

Beside him sat a young woman called Katherine Burgess, who had said she'd known him, briefly, when he'd had a name. But he wasn't sure of her, of her truth or her motivations. She had told him his real name was David and that he'd crewed on a Settler ship, but neither the name nor the classification seemed to fit as well as the identity he'd already been building for himself; so he continued to call himself by his chosen name, Derec, until he had solid proof of his other existence.

Flanking the humans on either side were two robots of advanced sophistication (Derec knew that, but didn't know how he knew it). One was named Euler, the other Rydberg, and they couldn't, or wouldn't, tell him any more than he already knew—nothing. The robots wanted information from him, however. They wanted to know why he was a murderer.

The First Law of Robotics made it impossible for robots to harm human beings, so when the only other human inhabitant of Robot City turned up dead, Derec and Katherine were the only suspects. Derec's brief past had not included killing, but convincing Euler and Rydberg of that was not an easy task. They were being held, but treated with respect—innocent, perhaps, until proven guilty.

Both robots had shiny silver heads molded roughly to human equivalent. Both had glowing photocells where eyes would be. But where Euler had a round mesh screen in place of a human mouth, Rydberg had a small loudspeaker mounted atop his dome.

"Do you enjoy this, Friend Derec?" Euler asked him, indicating the falling paper and the seemingly endless stream of robots that lined the route of their drive.

Derec had no idea of what he was supposed to enjoy about this demonstration, but he didn't want to offend his hosts, who were being very polite despite their accusations. "It's really . . . very nice," he replied, brushing a piece of paper off his lips.

"Nice?" Katherine said from beside him, angry. "Nice?"

She ran fingers through her long black hair. "I'll be a week getting all this junk out of my hair."

"Surely it won't take you that length of time," Rydberg said, the speaker on his head crackling. "Perhaps there's something I don't understand, but it seems from a cursory examination that it shouldn't take you any longer than . . ."

"All right," Katherine said. "All right."

". . . one or two hours. Unless of course you're speaking microscopically, in which case . . ."

"Please," she said. "No more. I was mistaken about the time."

"Our studies of human culture," Euler told Derec, "indicate that the parade is indigenous to all human civilizations. We very much want to make you feel at home here, our differences notwithstanding."

Derec looked out on both sides of the huge, open-air, V-shaped mover. The robots lining the streets stood quite still, their variegated bodies giving no hint of curiosity, though Derec felt it quite possible that he and Katherine were the first humans many of them had ever seen. Knowing nothing, Derec knew nothing of parades, but it seemed to be a friendly enough ritual, except for the paper, and it made him feel good that they should want him to feel at home.

"Is it not customary to wave?" Euler asked.

"What?" Derec replied.

"To wave your arm to the crowd," Euler explained. "Is it no customary?"

"Of course," Derec said, and waved on both sides of the machine that clanked steadily down the wide street, the robots returning the gesture with more nonreadable silence.

"Don't you feel like a proper fool?" Katherine asked, scrunching up her nose at his antics.

"They're just trying to be hospitable," Derec replied. "With the trouble we're in here, I don't think it hurts to return a friendly gesture."

"Is there some problem, Friend Katherine?" Euler asked.

"Only with her mouth," Derec replied.

Rydberg leaned forward to stare intently at Katherine's face. "Is there something we can do?"

"Yeah," the girl answered. "Get me something to eat. I'm starving."

Rydberg swiveled his head toward Euler. "Another untruth," he said. "This is very discouraging."

"What do you mean?" Derec asked.

"Our hypotheses concerning the philosophical nature of humanics," Rydberg said, "must have their foundation in truth among species. Twice Katherine has said things that aren't true . . ."

"I *am* starving!" Katherine complained.

". . . and how can any postulate be universally self-evident if the postulators do not adhere to the same truths? Perhaps this is the mark of a murderer."

"Now wait a minute," Derec said. "All humans make . . . creative use of the language. It's no proof of anything."

Rydberg examined Katherine's face closely. Then he pressed a pincer to her bare arm, the place turning white for a second before resuming its natural color. "You say you are starving, but your color is good, your pulse rate strong and even, and you have no signs of physical deterioration. I must conclude, reluctantly, that you are not starving."

"We are hungry, though," Derec said. "Please take us where we might eat."

Katherine fixed him with a sidelong glance. "And do it quickly."

"Of course," Euler said. "You will find that we are fully equipped to deal with any human emergency here. This is to be the perfect human world."

"But there are no humans here," Derec said.

"No."

"Are you expecting any?"

"We have no expectations."

"Oh."

Euler directed the spider-like robot guiding the mover, and the machine turned dutifully at the next corner, taking them down a double-width street that was bisected by a large aqueduct, whose waters had turned dark under the ever-deepening twilight.

Derec sat back and stole a glance at Katherine, but she was busily pulling bits of paper from her hair and didn't notice him. He had a million questions, but they seemed better left for later. As it was, he had conflicting emotions to analyze and react to within himself.

He was a nonperson whose life had begun scant weeks before, when he'd awakened without past or memory to find himself in a life-support pod, stranded upon an asteriod that was being mined by robots. They had been searching for something, something he had accidentally stumbled upon—the Key to Perihelion, at least one of the seven Keys to Perihelion. It had seemed of incredible import to the robots on the asteroid. Unfortunately, he had had no idea of what the Keys to Perihelion were or what to do with them.

After that was the bad time. The asteroid was destroyed by Aranimas, an alien space raider, who captured Derec and tortured him for information about the Key, information that Derec could not supply. There he had met Katherine, just before the destruction of Aranimas's vessel and their dubious salvation at the hands of the Spacers' robots.

The Spacers also wanted the Key, though their means of attaining it seemed slightly more civilized and bureaucratic than Aranimas's. Katherine and Derec were polite prisoners of bureaucracy for a time on Rockliffe Station, their personalities clashing until they were forced to form an alliance with Wolruf, another alien from Aranimas's ship, to escape their gentle captivity with the Key.

They found that if they pressed the corners of the silver slab and thought themselves away from the Spacer station, they were whisked bodily to a dark gray void that they assumed to be Perihelion. Pressing the corners again, another thought brought them to Robot City. And then their thinking took them no farther, stranding them in a world populated by nothing but robots.

And that was it, the sum total of Derec's conscious life. He had reached several conclusions, though, scant as his reserve of information was: First, he had an innate knowledge of robots and their workings, though he had no idea from where his knowledge emanated; next, Katherine knew more about him than she was willing to tell; finally, he couldn't escape the feeling that he was here for a purpose, that this was all some elaborate test designed especially for him.

But why? Why?

It was worlds that were being turned here, physical and spatial laws that were being forced upside down—all for him? Nothing made sense.

And then there was the Key, the object that everyone wanted, the object that was safely hidden by the person who couldn't control it. The robots here didn't know he had it. Were they looking for it, too? He'd have to find out. The Key seemed to be the one strain that held everything else together.

Keeping that in mind, he determined to move slowly, to try always to get more in the way of information than he gave. He'd been at a disadvantage for the entire length of his memory. From this point, he wanted to keep the upper hand as far as possible.

But there was, of course, the murder.

Derec stood on the balcony of the apartment given to him and Katherine by the robots, looking out over the night city. A stiff, cold wind had come up, the starfield totally obscured by dark, angry clouds that seemed to boil up out of nowhere. Lightning flashed in the distance, electrons seeking partner protons on the surface. It was a beautiful sight, and frightening. Derec watched the distant buildings light to near daytime before plunging once more into darkness.

"There," he said, pointing to a distant tower. "It wasn't there a centad ago."

Katherine walked up beside him, leaning against the balcony rail. "Where was it?" she asked, mocking.

"It wasn't anywhere," he replied, turning to take her by the shoulders. "It didn't exist."

"That's impossible," she replied, then turned and walked back into the large, airy apartment that sat at the top of another tower like the one Derec said had sprung from nowhere. "I wish they'd get here with our food."

"They're probably fixing us something extra special," Derec said, joining her in the living room. "And impossible seems to be the way of our lives right now, doesn't it? I'm telling you, Katherine, that along with everything else that doesn't make sense, this . . . city is growing, changing right before our eyes."

"How can that be?" she asked, and looked around uneasily. "I mean . . . cities are built, aren't they? They don't just grow."

Derec stared a circle around the room. It was hexagonal, like standing on the inside of a crystal, with no visible line of demarcation for the ceilings and floor. The furniture seemed to flow from the walls, as the table seemed to flow upward from the floor. Light concentrated from the ceiling and lit the room comfortably, but it seemed the ceiling itself that was alight, with no external apparatus to make it happen.

"Look around you," Derec said. "Everything's connected to everything else, and connected seamlessly. And it all seems to be made from the same material." He walked to a sofa that flowed out of the wall and sat on the cushion that formed its base. "Comfortable," he said, "but I think it's made from the same material as the harder stuff—some kind of steel and plastic alloy—just in different measure."

Katherine had walked to the table and was staring at it. "If you look closely," she said, "you can see a pattern to the material."

Derec stood and walked up beside her, leaning down on

the table to get a close look. The pattern was faint, but readable. The table was made up of a collection of trapezoidal shapes, interwoven and repeated over and over.

"Interesting," Derec said.

"How so?"

"Is the shape familiar to you?"

She narrowed her brows in concentration for a moment, then looked at him with wide eyes. "The same shape as the Key," she said.

He nodded.

Katherine left him standing there and hurried back out to the balcony.

"It's almost like individual pieces stuck together," he called to her. "I wonder how they connect . . ."

"It's gone!" she shrieked, and Derec hurried onto the balcony. "Your tower from before, it's gone!"

"No it's not," he said, pointing farther to the east.

"It's moved?"

He shook his head. "I don't think so." He pointed to the huge, pyramidal structure that dominated the landscape to the west. It was at the top of that place where they were first brought by the Key. "That's the only building I think doesn't change. And we couldn't see it from the balcony a moment ago."

"You mean, *we've* changed?"

"Something like that."

She put a hand to her head. "I didn't see . . . feel, I . . ."

"It's kind of like watching clouds," he said. "If you stare at them from moment to moment, they seem to be solid and stationary, but once you turn away and then look back, they've changed. It's almost like some sort of evolutionary growth . . ."

"In a building?"

"If you stay out there much longer, you will probably get wet," came a voice from behind them. They turned to see Euler's glowing eyes staring at them in the darkness.

"We've gotten wet before," Katherine returned, looking

past Euler to the food being set out on their table. "Ah, a last meal for the condemned."

"The rain here is particularly cool," the robot said, and watched as Katherine shoved past him and ran into the dining area, "perhaps uncomfortably cool for the human body temperature."

Thunder rumbled loudly in the distance, a brilliant shaft of lightning striking the top of the towering pyramid. Derec turned from the spectacle and moved toward the doorway, Euler stepping aside to let him pass.

He walked to the table, sitting across from Katherine, who was already piling food from a large golden bowl onto her plate, also gold-colored. The food seemed to be of a uniform, paste-like consistency, its color drifting somewhere between blue and gray. Golden cups filled with water sat beside the plates.

"Are these utensils made of gold?" Derec asked, clanging a spoon melodiously against his plate.

"Correct," Rydberg said. "It's a relatively useless soft metal that is a by-product of our mining operations. Its one major virtue besides its use as a conductor is the fact that it doesn't tarnish, making it ideal for human eating utensils. We made these things for David's visit."

Derec watched the serving spoon slip from Katherine's grasp to clang loudly against her plate. And for just a second her face turned white.

"That's what you told me *my* name was," Derec said, finding the coincidence a little too close for his comfort.

She fixed him with unfocused eyes, then shrugged, looking normal again. "It's a common enough name on Spacer worlds," she said, returning her attention to her plate.

She picked up the spoon and went back to the job at hand. Derec looked up at the robots who stood beside the table and the small servo Type-I:5 robot waiting patiently near the door for the return of the utensils.

"Would you care to sit with us while we eat?" Derec asked, and felt Katherine kick him under the table.

"Delighted," Euler said without hesitation, and the two robots sat at table attentively, apparently enjoying in their way the human familiarity.

Derec took the serving spoon and began filling his own plate. "I take it that David was the other human who came here?" he asked.

"That is correct," Rydberg said.

"Then he came in a ship?" Derec pressed.

"No," Euler said. "He simply walked into the city one day."

"From where?"

"I don't know."

"Aaaahhh!" Katherine yelled, spitting out food and grabbing for the glass of water, drinking furiously. The robots swiveled their heads to watch, then exchanged glances. "Are you trying to feed us or kill us?" she demanded.

"Our programming would never allow us to kill you," Rydberg said. "That would be quite impossible."

Derec tentatively dipped his spoon into the porridge-like mixture, taking a small bite. Not sour, not sweet, it simply had a strange, *alien* taste accompanied by a slight noxious odor, one he was also uncomfortable with.

"This stuff stinks!" Katherine said loudly, the robots looking at her, then turning expectantly toward Derec.

"She's right," Derec replied. "What is this?"

"A perfect, nontoxic mixture of local plant matter, high in protein and balanced carbohydrates," Rydberg said. "It's good for you."

"The other human ate this?" Derec asked.

"Quite enthusiastically," Euler said.

"No wonder he's dead," Katherine muttered. "This is simply unacceptable.. You're going to have to find us something else, something that tastes good."

Derec took another bite, this time holding his nose. Disassociating the smell from the food helped some, but not too much. The gruel left an unpleasant aftertaste. How could the other man have eaten it and not complained? Less made sense all the time.

"How long before you can get us something else?" Derec asked.

"Tomorrow?" Rydberg suggested. "Although they were proud of this in food services. Finding something of equal nutritional value will be difficult."

"Forget nutritional value to a degree," Derec said. "Study other human foods and see how well those can be duplicated exactly with the know-how you have here." He looked at Katherine. "We should probably try and choke some of this down to keep our strength."

She nodded grimly. "I'd already figured that," she said, and looked at Rydberg. "Bring me lots of water."

The robot hurried to comply, fetching a gold pitcher from the servo-cart and refilling her cup.

"When did he die, this David?" Derec asked, holding his nose and taking another bite.

"Seven days ago," Rydberg said, sitting again and carefully positioning the pitcher within everyone's easy reach on the table.

"Well, that rules us out as suspects then," Derec said happily. "We didn't arrive here until last night."

"You'll have to excuse me," Rydberg said politely, "but Katherine has already exhibited a penchant for speaking less than honestly—"

"What's that supposed to mean?" Katherine said angrily.

"No disrespect intended," Rydberg said. "It is simply the case that your veracity must be in question in light of our conversations of this afternoon. At this point, we don't know if we can trust anything either of you says."

"We don't even know where this place is," Derec said.

"Then how did you get here?" Euler asked, swiveling his head to stare directly at Derec.

"I . . ." Derec began, then stopped himself. He wasn't ready to admit any knowledge of the Key. It was their only weapon, their only potential salvation; he couldn't give it over so early in the game. "I don't know."

Rydberg stared for several seconds before saying, "To believe you means that you either materialized out of the ether or were somehow brought here totally without your knowledge or consent."

Derec responded by taking the conversation away from the robot's control. "You say this David also seemed to appear out of nowhere. Did you ever question him about his origins?"

"Yes," Euler said simply.

"And you know nothing about his background," Derec said, trying to keep his mind off the food by concentrating on the investigation. Across from him, Katherine was swallowing her food whole and washing it down with large gulps of water. "How was he dressed?"

"He was naked," Euler said. "And he stayed naked."

The two humans shared a look. Nudity was common and casual on many Spacer worlds, but the climate here would hardly recommend it. "When can we see the body?" Derec asked.

"That's not possible," Euler told her.

"Why?"

"I cannot tell you why."

"Cannot or will not?" Derec asked, exasperated.

"Cannot and will not," Euler replied.

"Then how do you expect us to investigate the cause of death?" Kate asked.

"If either or both of you are the murderers," Euler said, "you already know the cause of death."

"You've already decided our guilt," Derec said, pointing. "That's not fair or just."

"There are no other possibilities," Rydberg said.

"When the possible has been exhausted," Derec replied, "it is time to examine the impossible. We are innocent, and you can't prove that we aren't. It only follows that the death was caused by something else."

"Humans can murder," Euler said, as thunder crashed loudly outside. "Humans can lie. You are the only humans here, and murder has been done."

"We came out of nowhere," Derec returned. "So did David. Others could also have come out of nowhere, others you haven't discovered yet. Why, had we committed a murder, would we stay around for you to catch?"

The robots looked at one another again. "You raise logical questions that must be answered," Euler said. "We certainly sanction your investigation."

"How can we investigate without full access?"

"With all the other resources at your command," Rydberg said, then stood. "Are you finished eating?"

"For now," Derec said. "We'll want real food tomorrow, though."

"We will do our best," Euler said, and he, also, stood. "Until then, you will stay here."

"I thought I might go out," Derec said.

"The rains will come. It's too dangerous. For your own safety, you will stay here tonight. We have found that we cannot be certain if what you tell us is correct, so we're leaving a robot at the door to make certain you stay in."

"You don't know that we've done anything wrong. You can't treat us like prisoners," Katherine said.

"And we shall not," Rydberg said, moving toward the door; the servo whirred up to the table, its metal talons pulling the bowls and plates into its innards.

"There are many things we need to talk with you about," Derec said.

"Tomorrow will be the time," Euler said. "We will have a long interview at a prescribed time, where many issues will be discussed. Until then, we cannot fit it into our schedule. We are currently quite busy." The robots turned to go.

"A couple of questions first," Derec said, hurrying to put himself between the door and the robots. "You say we aren't prisoners, yet you have locked us up. How long do we have to stay in this place?"

"Until it is safe," Rydberg said.

"Then if you do let us out," Derec persisted, "how can you be sure we won't try to escape?"

"We will have to keep a very close watch on you," Euler replied.

With that, the robot firmly, but gently, pushed Derec aside and moved out the door, the servo following quickly behind. Derec tried to follow them out, but a squared-off utility robot blocked his path, its body streaked with random bands of different colored paints like the colors on an artist's pallet.

"Stand aside," Derec told the machine.

"It is dangerous for you outside. I am to keep you inside where it is safe, and have no more conversation with you lest you try and deceive me."

"Me?" Derec said. "Deceive?"

The robot pushed the door stud and the unit slid closed. Derec turned to Katherine. "What do you make of it?"

She moved to sit on the sofa, then stretched out, looking tired. "We're being held prisoner by a bunch of robots with no one in charge," she said, sighing deeply. "The dead man was an exhibitionist who could, apparently, eat anything. They want us to prove our innocence, but refuse to let us see the body or investigate." She sat up abruptly, eyes narrowing. "Derec, we've got to get out of here."

"They won't do anything to us without proof of our guilt," Derec replied. "It's not in their nature. We'll stay around and get this straightened out. Then they'll be happy to send us on our way. Besides, this place has got me really curious. How does it work . . . *why* does it work?"

She lay down again, staring at the ceiling. "I'm not so sure they'd really let us leave," she said, voice distant. "I think we've stumbled into something completely crazy. A robot world without humans could take any sort of bizarre turn."

"But not a . . . what did you say . . . completely crazy turn," he replied. "They can't be crazy; there's no logic to crazy. Besides, what makes you think we've stumbled into anything? We were brought here, plain and simple, for a reason that hasn't been made clear yet. Maybe a little time here will help us ferret it out."

"You ferret it out," she said. "I'm tired."

"Well, I'm not." He moved to the balcony, feeling the stiff wind on his face as the light show continued to rage outside. "I'm going out tonight and do a little poking around."

She was up from the couch, moving toward him. "They said it was dangerous," she said quietly, a hand going to his forearm. "Go out tomorrow."

"Under their watchful eye?" he said, then shook his head. "We need to get around on our own, and this is the time. Besides, a little rain can't hurt me."

"Stay," she said. "I'm afraid."

"You?" He laughed. "Afraid?"

She pulled her hand away. "All right," she said. "Go out and get yourself killed. I'm tired of looking out for you anyway."

"You're angry."

"And you're an idiot." She turned from him and stared out across the magnificent city, realizing that its beauty was for them alone to appreciate. There was something unutterably sad about that. "How will you get past the door guard?"

"We'll take his advice and deceive him," Derec said.

"We?"

"Will you help me?"

She turned and walked back into the apartment. "Anything to get you out of my hair," she said over her shoulder.

Derec's plan was simple enough, but it was one he could use only once. The robots learned quickly enough of human duplicity, arming themselves with the knowledge as a protection. But just this once, it might work.

He crouched beside the sofa, knotting into a tight ball. Just as soon as he was well out of sight of the door, Kate took a deep breath and tried to open it—locked.

She shrugged once in Derec's direction, then began screaming in terror. A second later the door slid open, the utility robot blocking the entry.

"What's wrong?"

"It's Derec!" she cried, pointing. "He fell from the balcony!"

Without hesitation, the robot rolled into the room, ready to check her story for lies and deceit. He quickly moved toward the balcony, leaning way over the edge to get a look into the night.

Derec jumped up from behind the couch and hurried quietly out the door and into the elevator that took him all the way to the ground and his first positive step in uncovering the mystery of Robot City. He was free, but what that meant here he could only guess.

Derec exited onto the wide street, hurrying across it to the shadows of buildings a half a block away. From there he took a few minutes to turn back and study the surroundings he had just left behind, trying to memorize the positions and shapes of the buildings near his tower. If his feelings were correct and the city was evolving outward, finding his way back could be a difficult, if not impossible, task. He didn't worry too much about it, though. He felt completely safe in this world of robots and figured that if he got lost, he'd simply turn himself in to the nearest robot of decent sophistication and be sent back.

That dwelt upon, he turned his attention completely to exploring the new world that an unseen fate had guided him to. In his current pristine state of innocence and awareness, it was difficult for Derec not to see the hand of destiny in his wanderings. It was as if his amnesia was an emotional and intellectual purging of sorts, set in motion to prepare him for a journey of which Robot City could be only a part. Since that was the only feeling or need he had to work with, he plunged himself into it with relish, enthusiasm, and as much good humor as he could muster. Katherine would never understand his feelings in this matter, but then Katherine had a life to go back to and memories to sustain her. For Derec, this was it, his whole world, and he wanted to know as much about it as he possibly could.

The city stretched all around him like some magnificent clockwork. The shapes of the buildings, from towering spires to squat storage warehouses, were all precise and multifaceted, like growing crystals. And the shapes seemed to be designed as much for aesthetic pleasure as pragmatic necessity. This concept formed the core of a theory within Derec's mind, and one that he would want to explore in greater detail when he had time for reflection. For nothing exists in a vacuum. Robots were not motivated independently by unreasoning emotion. They had to have reasons for their actions, and by what Derec had seen, their actions were all directed absolutely, despite Rydberg's claims of autonomy.

The cold winds sliced through him like a knife through water, and the sky rumbled and quaked, yet all around him he watched a furious activity that kept the mechanism of Robot City moving to its own internal rhythm and purpose. Hundreds of robots filled the streets around him, all moving and directed. All ignored his presence.

Streets were cleaned, even as spray painting was conducted on dull-sheened buildings, the sprayers held close to the target in the stiff wind—which probably explained the bands of paint on the utility robot that guarded the humans. Converted mining cars sped by, filled with broken equipment and scrap metal, their beamed headlights illuminating the streets before them like roving mechanical fireflies. Once he took to the shadows as a whole squad of drones, accompanied by a supervisor robot he hadn't seen before, drove past in an open-bed equipment mover and passed his position without a look before disappearing around a distant corner. He thought about following them, but decided that he would continue exploring slowly at first, getting a feel for his world and its parameters.

The questions in his mind seemed endless, and their answers only led to more questions. Who began Robot City, and why did the robots not know of their own origin? Why this place, this particular planet? Why a city of human proportions for a world of the nonhuman? Euler had called Robot City the perfect place for humans—why? The murder, to Derec, was nothing but a small nuisance with large complications. What really interested him was the motivation behind the city itself.

The lousy food raised a great many further questions in his mind. Spacer robots were designed solely as mechanical helpmates to human masters. Spacer robots *knew* how human beings reacted to food. The robots here had basic human knowledge and the Laws of Robotics as their core, yet remained ignorant of specific, conditioned reactions to humans. It was almost as if their design had geared them toward an equal human partnership, rather than a master/servant relationship, and they were feeling out their relationship with the animal called *human*. It was a dizzying concept to Derec, one that he'd also have to think out in greater detail.

And, finally, the dead man. Where did he fit into the picture . . . and why? Derec's mind, being a blank slate, soaked up everything around him like a sponge, unhampered by the intrusion of past thoughts and feelings that muddied observation. His eye for detail missed nothing, especially the reaction of Katherine to hearing Euler say the man's name—David.

What could it mean? He had literally stumbled upon Katherine, yet she seemed an indispensable part of the puzzle. What role did she play? Again, destiny seemed to rule the day—a place for everything, everything in its place. He was a blind man with a jigsaw puzzle, feeling his way through, groping sightlessly for the connections. He liked the girl, couldn't help it, and felt a strong physical attraction for her that he wouldn't even try to wish away; yet he couldn't shake the feeling that she was deeply involved in covering up his real identity and purpose. And again, his eternal question—why?

He continued moving down the street. Though the buildings were beautiful, they were nondescript, without markings of any kind. He recognized warehouses because parts were being moved in and out of them, but everything else seemed devoid of purpose. If he could find an official building, he could try to hook up to a terminal and make his own inquiries. The pyramid where he and Katherine had materialized, the place the robots called the Compass Tower, had seemed solid to him. Even though it appeared to be the point upon which all else hinged, he wasn't ready to go back to it yet.

The robots on the street ignored him as he moved through their midst. There seemed to be a sense of urgency to them that he couldn't understand. He stopped a utility robot like the one he had snuck past at the apartment, except this one had huge scoops for hands.

"Can you talk?" he asked.

"Yes, most assuredly," the robot answered.

"I need to find the administration building."

"I don't believe we have one here."

"Where would I find the closest computer terminal?"

"I regret that I cannot say."

Derec sighed. The runaround. Again. "Why can't you say?"

"If I told you that, you'd know everything."

"Know everything about what?"

"About the thing that I cannot talk about. If you'd like, you can stay here and I'll report to a supervisor and have him come out and find you."

"No, thanks," Derec replied, and the robot turned to walk away. "Hey, what's your hurry?"

"The rain," the utility said, pointing toward the sky. "The rain is coming. You had better get to shelter." The robot turned and hurried off, his box-like body weaving from side to side as he rolled along.

"What about the rain!?" Derec yelled, but his words were lost in a sudden gust of wind.

He watched the figure of the robot for a moment, realizing that the street he had come down looked different than it had a moment before. The whole block, street and all, had seemed to shift positions, bowing out to curve what had once been straight. A tall, tetrahedral structure, which he had used as a reference point, had disappeared completely. Ten minutes on the street and he was totally lost.

He pressed on, the wind colder now, more intense. If this was such a perfect world for humans, then why did the weather seem so bad?

He reached an unmarked corner and found himself on the street he had ridden down earlier, during the parade. It was extra wide, a large aqueduct bisecting it.

He moved to the edge of the aqueduct and stared down at the dark, rushing waters that filled it no more than a quarter full. Where had the waters come from? Where were they going? Had Robot City been built here for the water, or was the water somehow a consequence of the building?

The water rushed past, dark and inscrutable, much like the problem of Derec's past and, perhaps, his future. Yet he could know about the water. He could trace it to its source; he could follow it to its destination. He could *know*. The thought heartened him, for he could do the same with his life. Accepting that destiny and not chance had brought him to this impossible place, it then followed that the sources of that destiny could be traced through the city itself.

If he pursued it properly, he could trace the origins of the city and, hence, find his own origins. It seemed eminently logical, for he couldn't escape the concept that he and Robot City were inextricably linked, physically, emotionally, and, perhaps, metaphysically.

If his searching came to naught, at least he'd be keeping himself, keeping his blank mind, occupied. He'd begin with the water—trace it through source and destination, find out the why of it. He'd work on the robots, finding out what they knew, what they didn't know, what they'd be willing to tell him, and what he could find out from them unwillingly. And there was Katherine. He'd have to treat her like a friendly adversary and use whatever limited wiles he had at his disposal to find out her place in all this.

The water plopped below him, as if a large stone had been tossed in. He looked around but saw nothing save the gently glowing buildings and the distant robots hurrying about their secret business.

The water plopped again, farther down the aqueduct, then again, near the last place. He turned to stare in that direction when his shoulder was splashed by a drop of icy water.

A drop hardly described it. What hit him was more like a glassful. His jumpsuit sleeve was soaked, his shoulder cold. Water splashed on the street beside him, a drop bigger than a clenched fist, leaving a wet ring.

Derec had about a second to appreciate what was happening, for his mind to begin to realize what a major storm could mean, when the deluge struck.

With a force that nearly doubled him over, the rain fell upon Derec in opaque sheets that immediately cut off his field of vision. He was cold, freezing; the rain lashing him unmercifully, its sound a hollow roar in his ears.

He used his arms to cover and protect his head as the freezing downpour numbed his shoulders and back. He had to get to shelter quickly, but he had already lost his bearings in the curtian of water that surrounded him three-sixty.

He tentatively put out a foot, hoping he was moving in the direction of the buildings across from the aqueduct. Were he to move in the wrong direction, he'd fall into the aqueduct and be lost in its flowing waters.

Movement was slow as he felt his way, still doubled over, toward the buildings and safety. It seemed as if he should have reached them three times over—they couldn't have been more than ten meters distant—yet he hadn't gotten there yet. Could he have gotten turned the wrong way and simply be moving down the center of the street?

Keeping his balance was getting more difficult. Water on the street was up to his ankles, moving rapidly against his direction. He lost his footing and went to his knee, but managed to rise again. His clothes were now soaked through, and hung like icicles from his body. Every step was a labor.

"The perfect world," he muttered, a thin smile stretching his lips despite his predicament.

Just as he was about to give up on his present direction and pick another one at random, the hulk of a building began to define itself in his vision. A few more treacherous steps and he was suddenly out of the rain, standing beneath a short awning that overhung the building front.

He used a hand to wipe the water from his face, then hugged himself, shivering, against the damp cold, taking stock of his position. The overhang protected the building front only for about a meter, and it extended for perhaps three meters in either direction from where he stood.

Beyond the awning, he could see nothing. The roaring water was impenetrable. The building front was no better. It was totally blank, no doors or windows. Yet, oddly enough, when he touched it, it felt warm, resisting the chill of the air. He was stuck in a world one meter wide by five meters long. The ground water had risen from his ankles to his calves, its current always pulling at him.

He stood there for several minutes, cold, teeth chattering, cursing the fate that would bring him to this hellhole. His numbness and melancholy soon, inevitably, turned to anger.

"Damn you!" he screamed, to whom, to what, he didn't know. "Why me?"

In frustration, he turned to the wall behind him. Hands balled into fists, he pounded viciously at the wall and—his hands sank right into it!

"Aaaahh!"

He screamed in surprise, instinctively jumping backward.

The water cascading from the awning caught him on the face, and as he tried to duck away from it, the ground current took him down.

He went under, then came up gasping for breath. But his control was gone and he was caught in the current. It pulled him back across the street; even the street itself seemed tilted at an angle toward the aqueduct. At this point, trying to regain his footing was out of the question. Keeping his head above water was the only priority. Staying alive was everything.

He felt himself go over the lip of the aqueduct and plunge into its raging waters. He bobbed down, at no point touching bottom, then rose again, totally numb and choking as the swift current carried him away, pulling at him, sucking him ever down.

He had wanted to see the terminal point of the waters. He would now see it quickly—if he could stay alive long enough.

Katherine stood with Euler by the opening to the balcony, staring out at a completely opaque wall of water that made her think that Robot City didn't really exist at all, but was simply an image conjured by an overactive brain exposed to too much cosmic radiation. The rain came down in never-ending torrents, rain such as she'd never seen or even thought could exist. It frightened her, a fright that almost overcame her anger at their predicament. Almost.

"Why did he go out?" Euler asked.

"I've already told you," she replied, turning away from the incredible downpour and moving back into the apartment. "He wanted to see the city."

"But we told him it was dangerous."

Katherine sat on the couch, folding her arms across her chest. A black hole could swallow Derec *and* his robots for all she cared. "He either didn't believe you or didn't care," she said. "Why are you standing here asking me the same thing over and over when you could be out there looking for him?"

Rydberg came in from the bedroom, where he had apparently been searching in case Katherine had been lying. "Everything that can be done is being done," he said. "We appreciate your concern. Ours is every bit as great as yours."

"I'm not concerned," she said. "I couldn't care less."

The robots exchanged glances. "You don't care about the possible loss of a human life?" Euler asked.

Katherine jumped up from the couch. "You mean he could possibly be . . . be . . . ?"

"Dead?" Rydberg helped. "Of course. We warned you that it was dangerous."

For the fiftieth time since Derec's leaving, she hurried back to the balcony doorway and stared into the blank wall of water. He'd been gone for several hours, far longer than he should have been. If anything had happened to him—

"Why did he go out?" Euler asked from beside her.

"Again!" she said loudly. "That same question. Why do you keep asking me that?"

"Because we don't understand," Rydberg said, moving up to join them. "You must know that robots don't lie."

"Yes," she replied.

"Then, when we said it was dangerous, why did he risk his life?" Euler asked.

"To begin with, his definition of danger might be different from yours," she said. "But beyond that, he wanted to know about this crazy city of yours more than he was afraid of the danger."

"You mean," Euler said, "that he could have purposely risked his life just for the sake of curiosity?"

"Something like that."

"Astounding."

"Let me ask you a question," she said, poking Euler in his chest sensors with an index finger. "If you want people to live here so much, why did you pick a place with such dangerous weather?"

Rydberg seemed to hesitate, as if he were weighing the answer he was about to give by some sort of internal scale. "The weather here is not naturally like this," he said at last.

"Naturally," she repeated, zeroing in on the key word. "Does this mean that something has affected the weather adversely?"

"Yes," Euler said.

"What?" she asked.

"We cannot tell you that," Rydberg said, and walked over to peer beneath the couch.

"Will it stop soon?" Kate asked.

"Probably within the next hour," Euler said. "At which time we can conduct an extensive search for Friend Derec."

A thought struck Katherine. She wanted to suppress it, but couldn't. "Is this how the other man . . . David, died?"

"He may have caused the rains," Euler said. "but he didn't die from them."

"I don't understand."

"It is quite late for humans," Rydberg said, moving toward the door. "You must sleep now or risk damaging your health."

With that, the two supervisor robots moved silently into the hallway, the door sliding shut behind them.

Katherine was alone, except for the robot standing guard in the hallway outside. She moved to the couch and curled into a tight ball. "Oh, David," she cried into the sleeve of her jumper. "Why did this have to happen?"

Derec rode the aqueduct like a log in a sluice, his body numb, his senses and his fate out of control. The waters raged in his ears as his entire existence turned on the simple act of trying to keep his head above water. Nothing else mattered; life had reduced itself to its essence. There was no fear, no time for it, and any yearnings to have his life pass before his eyes went unsatisfied, since he had no life to reflect upon. There was only the water and the numbing cold—and the ubiquitous companionship of Death.

His ride could have lasted a minute or an eternity—he was beyond calculating time—but when he felt himself freefalling in midair, his brain snapped to the new reality and questioned.

He was falling, surrounded by a hot, moist wind. A bare glow of light seemed to envelope him, but before he had a chance to appreciate it, he splashed into hot water.

He had gulped down water with his quickly sucked breath, and when he bobbed to the surface like a cork, he was choking and coughing, his head pounding with a heartbeat throb. He panicked, then forced himself into control when he realized the water he was in wasn't flowing, but pooling.

As he treaded water, he found himself grateful to his former life for giving him the lifesaving advantage of swimming lessons. He leaned back and floated on his back, small currents pulling him this way and that. His body ached horribly from the battering he had taken in the aqueduct; every bit

27

of strength had drained from him.

There was a ceiling of some sort above him, tiny lights making it dimly visible. The roar of waterfalls filled the hollow cavern completely, and he turned his head to the side to get a glimpse of his surroundings.

He was a hundred meters from the edge of a large square pool that stretched perhaps a thousand meters across. Red lights set at regular intervals bathed the entire area in an eerie glow. In the middle of each side of the pool were aqueduct runoffs, four in all, their cascades shimmering like fading pulsars in the red haze. These four runoffs provided the incredible noise that churned inside his head, all of it echoing within the confined space.

Where was he? A collection point of some kind, perhaps a reservoir. Any city needed a water supply. This was probably connected to a water treatment plant meant to sustain the human population that didn't live there. This only strengthened Derec's earlier speculation that this was not a city simply meant for robots. What was going on here was serious colonization.

Another realization occurred to him, too. The reservoir had saved his life. He had been showing the beginning signs of hypothermia during his wild ride down the aqueduct, but the hot water of the reservoir was thawing him out.

Why hot water? The water was definitely warmer than human body temperature, perhaps as much as fifteen degrees, and incredibly hot winds were raging through the chamber, competing with the charging runoff waters in loudness. In fact, the soothing heat and the rest were already beginning to lull his senses, and he realized that if he wasn't careful, he could end up at the other end of the physical spectrum with hyperthermia. Whether hypo or hyper, though, the results were still the same. He was going to have to get out of the water or risk overburdening his heart.

Still on his back, he churned his legs lightly while propelling himself with his arms. There seemed to be robotic movement at the far end of the reservoir, but he didn't have the strength to swim that far. Having no idea of which way to go, he simply moved toward the closest shoreline. The process was time-consuming, though, for the runoffs created their own currents.

He swam with leisure, but determination, taking the time to check out his body. He had taken a beating in his wild ride down the aqueduct, but besides general bruises, nothing major seemed to be wrong.

As he neared the edge of the pool, he could see that the runoff streams had slowed considerably, leading him to speculate that the rain had stopped outside. Fuzzy light was also beginning to seep in around the dark edges of the covered pool, and he realized that day had broken.

He finally reached the edge of the pool, its surface made from the same material as the rest of the city. Metal ladders were set at regular intervals around the edge, and he floated to the nearest one to begin his climb out.

The water was barely three meters from the top of the pool, and fortunately so, because as soon as Derec began his climb he knew he wasn't doing well. His body, so light in the water, felt like it weighed a ton. The combination of emotional stress, the ordeal of the aqueduct, and the overheated water of the pool had all had an effect on his body. He dragged himself slowly up the ladder, then rolled, gasping, onto the edge of the pool and lay there.

He closed his eyes, just for a minute, and he was gone. He didn't know how long he had slept, but when he awoke, it was with a start. A loud rumble assailed his hearing. He sat up quickly, darting his head around, and saw a large vehicle moving around the pool toward him, its engine noises amplified to a roar in the cavern-like surroundings.

Standing was a problem, since Derec still felt weak. But he got up on shaky legs and moved toward the areas of light beyond the reservoir. While he was still out and on the loose, he wanted to see as much as he could. For, this time, the robots wouldn't be so quick to let him out of their sight.

As he moved toward the light, he passed open caverns

that were filled with conduits for moving water. The huge pipes were twisted like knotted rope and seemed to be moving, writhing, like a snake pit—almost as if they were alive. He was taken over these areas by railed walkways that simply extended from the edges of the pit at his approach, growing—like crystals—before his eyes.

After the pits, he passed several squat buildings where he surmised the actual water treatment was performed. Drone robots moved in and out of the facilities rapidly, mostly moving machinery in both directions. Derec briefly considered going into one of the structures to search for a terminal, but the still-approaching vehicle made him change his mind.

"HUMAN!" came a loudspeakered voice. "YOU WILL HALT YOUR PROGRESS WHERE YOU ARE. IT IS UNLAWFUL FOR YOU TO PROCEED."

He turned to the sound. It was coming from the robot-controlled vehicle that was rapidly closing the distance on him. It was time to move!

He ran past the buildings toward glowing walls of light just beyond.

"HUMAN!" the loudspeaker called again.

He raced to the wall, his legs heavy. The entire wall seemed lit and wrapped a circle around the reservoir area. It was translucent, like a shower curtain, and he realized that it was simply so thin that outside light passed right through. He pushed on it, but it felt solid. He pushed harder, and it gave under his hand, just like the wall last night.

Just then, he saw a drone approach the wall twenty meters distant and move right through it. He hurried there, with the robots in the vehicle closing rapidly on him. He stood at the spot, seeing no entry, but when he raised his hands to push against it, the wall irised open and he stepped through into the daylight.

It was morning, bright and calm, with no sign of the deluge that had taken place the previous night. The sun was still low in the sky, but Robot City was alive and active.

He was in the very heart of it here, the hub upon which

the wheel of the city turned. He could see the aqueduct that had brought him cutting through the city like a spoke, and he could see other aqueducts, other spokes, slicing through the wheel of the city. And he began to think of the areas between the spokes as quadrants.

Robots in large numbers hurried quickly through the streets, always going somewhere, always busy with predetermined tasks. Many of them were disappearing into the treatment plant.

He moved a small distance from his exit point, then looked back at the reservoir, shocked to find a forest there! Then he realized that the forest had been planted above the reservoir, the land area serving double duty. But why a forest? Not for robots, certainly.

Out of the corner of his eye, he noticed the large, wheeled vehicle that had been tracking him within the reservoir moving through the exit point to the outside. He looked back at the city, then up at the forest. He would find escape in its random chaos.

Angling himself away from his pursuers, he ran back toward the huge reservoir building, preparing to climb one of the struts that helped support the outside edge of the forest. But as soon as he reached the place and put his hands on the arched strut, it seemed to melt away, changing into a gently sloping stairway.

He hurried up the stairs without a question and entered the forest. The ground was moist and spongy, muddying his already-soaked shoes. The trees were small, in many cases smaller than the underbrush that grew thick around them. A haze seemed to fill the entire forest, and the farther he plunged into it, the hazier it became.

Derec was no expert in vegetation, but he assumed the trees were all offspring, many generations removed, of trees that had once grown on Earth. Spacers, though hating to mention any connection to the planet of their ancestry, nevertheless made it a point to bring Earth vegetation and animal life to whatever planet they colonized. Where he'd gotten such information, he had no idea; the small glimpses of his own mind were maddening in their incompleteness.

He wandered the forest, pushing through the haze and the dense undergrowth, feeling jittery in untamed surroundings. And he knew that these were also the feelings of a Spacer pushing through his mind. He didn't much like the forest; he longed for the order of the city. But for a human being, this had its place. Untamed but finite, aesthetically pleasing without being uncontrollable. This place existed for the aesthetics—for human aesthetics.

His foot hit something hard and uncompromising, and he tripped, going hard to soft ground, getting mud all over himself. He turned to the object that had caused his fall and found a small section of pipe sticking out of the ground. A fog-like haze was pumping from the pipe, the same haze that filled the entire area, and Derec began to see a master plan at work here.

He stood, then ducked when he saw a shadow moving through the haze not five meters from him. It was one of the robots. He listened and could hear them thrashing through the brush all around. They were slowly cordoning off the entire area, boxing him in.

He took a deep breath, then scrunched up into a ball and lay on the ground, listening as they moved near him. The forest was built over the reservoir so that condensing water could feed up to the trees from beneath and nourish the roots directly. Further, the haze was probably carbon dioxide vapor feeding the forest to promote health and growth. Where did the CO_2 come from? Perhaps a bleed-off from their industrial processes, which could also explain the heat in the reservoir area. The set-up was sophisticated and civilized, a city built around its ecological needs. Was it all of robot design?

A metal foot clanked down just an arm's reach away from his position. He stifled the urge to rise up for a breath of normal air. Within seconds, the robot moved on.

As he heard the search party sweep past, he jumped to his

feet and charged back in the direction he had come. The robots were much faster and stronger than he was, so he was going to have to make things happen quickly at this point.

He reached the edge of the forest in minutes, and rushed to the place where he had climbed up. The strut was already solid again, the steps nowhere to be seen. He looked over the edge of the forest. It was ten meters to the ground; jumping was out of the question.

"You, Derec!" came a robot voice behind. "Stop now! Stop!"

He sat on the ground and dangled his legs over the edge of the strut. Steps miraculously formed again. He ran down just as several robots reached the edge of the forest, calling for him to stop.

Amidst the confusion near the water treatment facility, he saw a large flatbed vehicle, filled with what looked like broken computers, ready to pull out. He took the last steps in leaps and charged the machine, the robots behind already reaching the bottom of the stairs.

The truck pulled out before he reached it, but with a burst of speed, he caught it and jumped into the back. A small, round drone the size of his head squeaked at him from among the broken computers.

Katherine stood at the wash basin, watching the lukewarm water flow from the tap, and wondered how plumbing could possibly be accomplished in a city that didn't stand still. She splashed her face with water, then stared into the small mirror that was inset above the basin. Her eyes were puffy and dark, showing the results of no sleep, but her face remained calm, remarkably calm considering the terror that had been flashing through her for most of the long night.

He was gone, perhaps dead, and she was alone on this crazy world. Though David/Derec, whatever he wanted to call himself, had never looked on this place as anything but an adventure, to her it had been nothing but a prison. A first priority for anyone marooned in a Spacer port would be access to radio communications to inform search parties and anxious waiters; yet the robots seemed reluctant—no, evasive—when it came to the topic of communications. That frightened her more than anything else that was going on.

"Did you sleep well?"

She jumped to the sound, turning quickly to see Rydberg standing in the doorway, a light static issuing from his loudspeaker.

"I didn't invite you in here!" she said in anger and frustration. "Get out! Now!"

The robot turned without a word and moved from the door, Katherine following him out into a small hallway.

"What do you want?" she asked. "Has there been any . . . news about Derec?"

Rydberg turned back to her. "I did not mean to intrude upon your privacy," he said. "Please accept my apologies. I've brought you food."

"I'm not hungry."

Rydberg just stared at her.

"Has there been any word about Derec?" she asked again, softly this time.

"Yes," the robot replied. "He was seen not three decads ago, but ran away when another of our supervisors called to him."

She clapped her hands together loudly. "So, he's alive!"

"Apparently so. Why would he run away? Is this a sign of guilt?"

"It's a sign that he wants to check out this crazy place without a gaggle of robots hanging all over him." She moved past him toward the living room. "Now, where's that food? I'm so hungry I could eat a . . ." She stopped herself, then looked at the robot. "I'm hungry."

"But you just said . . ."

"Forget what I just said. Correction!" She caught herself before the robot could explain its memory. "I mean never mind. Where's the food?"

He led her back down the hall to the living room, where the food sat at the same table she had eaten at the night before. Strangely enough, the room was different, squatter, wider than it had been the previous night, the table closer to the wall.

She moved quickly to the table. There was a variety of what appeared to be fruits and cooked vegetables there. She sat down and tentatively ate a small piece of greenish fruit. It was delicious. Rydberg stood nearby as she greedily sampled everything on the table, all of it good. She didn't invite the robot to sit with her as Derec had done. The machines were servants and needed to be treated as such. She'd never understand his insistence on treating them as anything other than the machines they were.

"When do we get to make outside radio contact?" she asked once the initial hunger pangs had died down.

"We will all meet later and discuss those questions."

"Are you going to put us on trial," she asked, "for the murder of this other human? We are entitled to a trial, you know."

"Derec has told us that he will try to solve this mystery," Rydberg said.

Katherine stopped eating and stared at him. "And what if he doesn't? What if we don't *ever* discover what really happened? You have no right to hold us here as it is. We can't go on indefinitely like this."

"If he cannot find out the truth of the matter," Rydberg said, "then we will assume our original supposition to be correct."

"I don't believe you," she said. "You have no right to determine my guilt or innocence without proper evidence. I'm not Derec, and I hold no romantic visions of a robot-controlled world. You cannot be allowed to have any power over the way I live my life. If you want to hold me for murder, you must put me on trial and prove it. If you put me on trial, I must be allowed to defend myself. I therefore demand immediate access to a radio so that I may provide myself with proper defense representation. I want a certified legal rep, and I want one now!"

"We will discuss the situation later today," the robot said, "after Friend Derec has been returned to us. Meanwhile, your food is getting cold and will lose its appeal."

"It already has," Katherine returned, pushing the plate away from herself. She didn't like the way this was turning. The radio seemed to get more and more distant to her, and with it, any hopes of ever leaving this place. Her arguments to Rydberg were based solely on laws and customs common to Auroran society. But all law, all freedom, was merely a rationalization away where a robot civilization was concerned.

The final result to her was quite simple: the machines were in charge and they could do anything they wanted.

Derec knew nothing with which to compare the size of Robot City, but as he drove its breadth, he couldn't help but feel its vastness.

As the parts truck moved quickly through the city streets, the round drone bounced from one machine to another, squeaking loudly, its silver body lighting up in dozens of places, then winking out again as it performed automatic (but definitely sub-robotic) pre-troubleshooting functions on the broken machinery. Finally, it came to rest on Derec's lap, all of its lights blinking madly, its squeaks turning into a high-pitched whine.

"So, where are we going?" he asked the troubleshooter while idly stroking its dome.

The machine whirred and bounced, but never answered. All at once, its whine turned to a loud, siren-like wail.

"Stop it!" Derec ordered, turning to the front of the truck to make sure he wasn't attracting attention. He bent double over the thing, trying to muffle its sound without success.

"You're going to have to stop," he told the thing. "I can't just . . ."

It sent a jolt of electricity through its body, shocking Derec, moving him off.

"All right," he said, pointing a shaking finger at the silver ball. "I don't have to take that from you."

The thing started bouncing up and down, higher and higher. Derec looked both ways over the truck back, then calmly brought up a foot and shoved the thing right off the truck, where it hit the street angrily, its wail louder as it bounced around like a rubber ball.

Within a few blocks, the vehicle slowed its pace, then got in line behind several other trucks, all filled with equipment. Derec got on his knees and looked over the piles of computers.

The trucks were pulled up to a gate, where a whole line of robots were moving up to the truck back, each taking a single piece of equipment and returning with it to a blockhouse that wasn't much larger than a single doorway. Beside the blockhouse was the most amazing thing Derec had ever seen in his short memory.

A huge, gray machine rumbled softly, yet with undeniable strength and power. From it issued what could only be described as a ribbon of city. In five-meter-square slabs, the city appeared to be simply extruding from underground through the medium of the gray machine.

It pushed itself along, the slabs gradually forming and reforming as they moved, following some incredible preprogramming that actually let them *build* themselves. And as the slabs formed walls and floors and corners and stories and windows, they spun off in every direction in a slow, graceful dance that pushed against the already existing buildings, the mechanism that triggered the entire magnificent clockwork of Robot City.

It was as if the entire city were one mammoth, living organism always growing outward, always changing and replicating like the cells in a body, moving in imprinted patterns toward a complete, fully formed being.

It was a plan of monumental scale, an atmosphere of total,

logical control for a given end. As he watched a skyscraper literally build itself from the ground up, each story pushing up the story above it and self-welding according to some unseen plan, he experienced the grandeur of an idea so vast that his limited knowledge was humbled by its power. This civilization was the product of a mind that refused to believe in limited options, a mind that accepted that what the imagination could conceive, the hands could make.

To such a mind, anything was possible. Even, perhaps, Perihelion.

The truck lurched, nearly knocking him from his knees. It had pulled up to the gate. The line of robots was now reaching into *his* bed for their equipment.

If all the action was happening below ground, that's where Derec wanted to be. Hurrying out of the truck, he grabbed a small terminal that looked as if it had been shorted out by water, and took his place behind a robot heading toward that doorway into the ground.

He reached the doorway, cradling the computer like a baby. Warm air greeted him as he stepped through into barely lit darkness. He was confronted by a short flight of stairs leading down, and followed the robot that walked down before him.

The stairs terminated in a large holding area, brightly lit, frenetic with activity. Automated carts carried robots and mining equipment at breakneck pace. The cars zipped around one another in seemingly rehearsed fashion, their movements perfected over time, since it seemed impossible to Derec that they could move so quickly without hitting one another.

On the far wall sat a bank of elevators, perhaps twenty in all, some of them remarkably large. The robots that moved down the stairs headed toward these elevators, apparently going from here to a lower level where repair or scrap work was being done.

Having no idea of where to go, Derec chose an elevator at random and moved toward it with his burden. A large elevator nearby slid open, and a group of minerbots, covered with mud and soot, moved out bearing the non-operating carcass of one of their own above their shoulders.

Derec reached the elevator. It had no formal controls, but opened for him as soon as he stepped near.

A voice boomed behind him. "Nothing awaits you below, but death!"

He turned to see a huge supervisor robot, twice the size of a man, glaring down at him with red photocells. The robot's body was burnished a bright, shimmering black.

"I've come to inspect your operation," Derec said, feigning authority. He turned back to the elevator and began to step in.

The robot's arm flashed out, his mammoth pincers clanging loudly around Derec's forearm, squeezing tightly but not painfully.

"You are caught," the machine said, and Derec's computer crashed loudly at his feet.

CHAPTER 4
THE COMPASS TOWER

As the door to the apartment slid open, Derec tucked under the arm of the big robot, watched Katherine's facial expression change from horror, to relief, to unbridled amusement —all in the space of three seconds.

"Let me guess," she said, putting a finger to her lips, "you're a ditty bag."

"Cute," Derec returned as the robot set him gently on the ground. He looked up at the huge, black machine. "Thanks for the ride, Avernus."

"My pleasure, Friend Derec," the robot replied, bending slightly so that the hallway could accommodate his height. "But I must ask you to stay away from the underground. It is no place for a human."

"I appreciate your concern," Derec said noncommittally. He walked into the apartment, then turned back to Avernus. "Will we see you at the meeting?"

"Most assuredly," he returned. "All of us look forward to it with great expectation."

"You can go now," Katherine told Avernus coldly, the robot nodding slightly and moving off, the utility robot guard sliding quickly to fill the door space with his squat body.

Katherine punched the door stud, the panel sliding closed. "You missed breakfast *and* lunch," she said, moving to sit listlessly on the couch.

"Avernus got me something before he brought me back,"

Derec said. "He got my wounds cleaned up, and even let me sleep for a while." Finally, he couldn't ignore her mood any longer. "What's wrong?"

"You," she said, "this place . . . everything. I don't know which way is up anymore. Did you find out anything?"

Derec spotted the CRT screen set up on the table and walked to stand before it. "It's a place designed for humans," he said, "and the building is going on at a furious pace, as if they're in some kind of hurry to get finished. I think the buildings may be . . . I don't know, alive, I guess is the best way to put it." He pointed to the screen. "Where did this come from?"

"Rydberg brought it," she answered, "But it only receives. What do you mean, the city's alive?"

"Watch this," Derec said, and ran full speed across the room, banging into the far wall. The wall gave with him, caving inward, then gently pushed itself back to a solid position.

"I laid awake all night worrying about you, while you were discovering the walls are made of rubber?" she asked loudly.

He turned to her, smiling. "Did you *really* worry about me?"

"No," she replied. "What else?"

He walked over and sat on the couch with her, his tones hushed. "I saw the city building itself, literally extruding itself from the ground. I tried to go down there, but Avernus caught me. I think he's in charge down there. The only thing I can figure is that there are immense mining operations underway below ground and that the buildings are positronic, some kind of cellular robots that make up a complete whole. It's fascinating!"

Katherine was unimpressed. "Did you find a way out of here?"

He shook his head. "Not yet," he answered, "but I don't really think that's going to be a problem."

"That's because you're so eaten up with your robot friends you *can't* think of anything else!" She suddenly jerked her head toward the wall. "If the walls are robots, I wonder if they can hear us now?"

Just then the screen on the table came to life, Rydberg's face filling it. "So, you are back, Derec," he said. "Good. Prepare yourselves. An honor guard is coming right now to bring you to your preliminary trial."

"Trial?" Derec said.

"Uh oh," Katherine said, putting a hand to her mouth. "That may be my fault. I all but dared them to put us on trial."

"But we haven't had a chance to investigate yet."

She shrugged. "I was trying to find if we could have access to outside communications." She snapped her fingers. "Maybe this means we're going to get it."

"Yeah . . . maybe," Derec said, but he was skeptical. Robot City was too precious a gem to be hanging out in the ether for anyone to pluck. At this point, he wasn't even sure if he *wanted* to communicate with the outside.

He looked at the screen. It had already gone blank. "Whatever the reason," he said, "I believe we're going to get some answers at this point."

"Let's hope they're answers we can live with," she sighed. "I don't want to spend the rest of my life here."

Within minutes, the utility robot was knocking on the door. Derec hurried to open it. Euler greeted him, accompanied by a supervisor robot he'd not seen before. This one was the robot most closely molded to a human that Derec had seen, with chiseled, though blank, mannequin-like features.

"Friend Derec," Euler said, "Friend Katherine Burgess, may I present Arion, who will be in attendance at our meeting."

"Pleased to meet you," Derec said.

"Rydberg called it a trial," Katherine said.

"This is a great moment for us here," Arion said. "I trust that your stay so far has been satisfactory. I am doing my best with what little time I have to try and prepare some entertainment for you. We know that humans enjoy mind diversions."

"We'd appreciate anything you could do," Derec said.

"Sure," Katherine said. "How about conjuring up a radio for us to call the outside for help?"

"Oh, that's quite impossible," Arion said.

"That's what I thought," Katherine answered.

"I have a present for each of you," Euler said, extending his right arm. "Then we must be off to the meeting."

Derec moved to the robot. His pincers held two large watches, dangling on gold chains. "You may know the time here now," Euler said. "It is of importance to humans, and so, to us. We will do more to make you feel comfortable in this regard."

Derec took the watches, giving one of them to Katherine. They had square faces encased in gold. On both of them, the LCD faces read 3:35. "They run on a twenty-four hour day," said Euler. "We thought it would be more comfortable for you if we adjusted the length of our hour than if you had to adjust to a twenty-and-one-half hour day. Our hours, decads, and centads are approximately eighty-five percent of standard." Derec walked out onto the veranda and looked into the sky. The sun had already passed its apex and was slowly crawling toward the eventual shadows of evening.

"Right on the money," he said, returning to the apartment.

"You doubted it?" Arion asked, looking at Euler.

"Do you understand now?" Euler said to him.

"Interesting," Arion said, cocking his head in an almost human fashion.

"We must go," Euler said and hurried out of the apartment, the others following.

They rode the elevator to street level and boarded a multi-car tram that had no apparent driver. It started off immediately when they were seated. Euler turned to Derec, who sat, with Katherine, behind him and Arion. "You put yourself in extreme danger last night," the robot said. "Why?"

"I've a better question," Derec returned. "If this is such a perfect human world, why was it so dangerous?"

"Spacer worlds conquered weather problems eons ago," Katherine interjected. "For you to have them in such an advanced culture makes no sense."

Arion turned to her and bowed his head. "Thank you for calling our culture advanced."

"The weather," Euler said, "is quite honestly part of our overall problem right now. It is under our control, but also not under our control. Unfortunately, for security reasons, we cannot discuss it in detail."

"Great," Katherine said. "Everybody can do something about the weather, but nobody talks about it."

"To answer your original question," Derec told Euler, as he watched them move in a direct line toward the tower where they had initially materialized, "I have no memory and no past. My curiosity, my search for answers about myself, leads me to do things not necessarily in my best interest."

"Amnesia?" Euler asked. "Or something else?"

Derec looked at him in surprise. "What else?"

The robot answered his question with another question, an old one. "How, then, did you come to our planet?"

Derec realized that the robot was playing word games with him that tied directly to the word games Derec had initiated the night before. He decided to keep playing. "What did the dead man, David, say when you asked him that question?"

"He said he didn't know," Euler replied, and turned back around in his seat. Over his shoulder, he said, "He claimed he'd had amnesia."

The tram came to a halt beside the mammoth pyramid that dominated the landscape of Robot City, the place the inhabi-

tants called the Compass Tower. Katherine put a hand on
Derec's arm, squeezing, and he knew she had the same fear
that he'd felt. Here, about halfway up the tower, was where
they had hidden the Key to Perihelion that had brought them
to the city. Had the robots found it? Were they confronting
them with the evidence, or, worse yet, taking it away?

But Euler said nothing of the Key. Instead, he simply
climbed from the tram and led them directly to the base of
the tower, a tower that Derec had surmised was solid.

He'd never been more wrong.

At the robot's approach, an entire block of the solid matter
that formed the base simply melted away, leaving a gently
sloping runway leading into the structure, another example
of Derec's theory about the intelligence of the building materials themselves.

They moved into the pyramid through a short, dark hallway that emptied into a maze of criss-crossing aisles and
stairs that, in turn, led off in all directions within the structure.

"Try and memorize our path," Derec whispered to Katherine. "Just in case."

"In case of what?" she asked. "In case you haven't figured
it out, we're not going anywhere."

"This is the most important building in our city," Euler
said, as he took them up a series of stairs and escalators that
zig-zagged at every landing and culminated in a long, well-
lit hallway. "This is where decisions are made, where . . .
understanding takes place."

They walked the hall, Arion hurrying ahead and disappearing down some stairs. The surrounding walls glowed
lightly, with connecting hallways intersecting every ten feet.

They followed Arion's path, changing direction several
times before finding themselves standing in a large, well-lit
room whose four walls angled in toward a ceiling, fifteen
meters above, that poured in sunshine like a skylight.

The floor of the room was tiled in the form of a large

compass, its four points forming the cornerstones of Robot City. In the center of the compass, under the direct rays of the sun, stood six robots in a circle, arms outstretched, their pincers grasping those of their neighbors on either side with space left for one more—Euler.

"This is the place where we seek perfection," Euler said, and joined the circle, closing it.

"It's almost religious," Derec whispered to Katherine.

"Yeah," she replied. "It give me the creeps."

Derec looked around the room. There were no chairs or tables, nothing upon which a human being could rest. The walls were inset with CRTs jammed side to side around the entire perimeter. Each screen showed its own view of Robot City. Many showed excavation sites, the large movers pushing and leveling soil. Other pictures were of the extrusion plant he had visited, and he was led to conjecture that there might be more than one. There were pictures of the reservoir he had splashed into, and strange, underground pictures taken through the eyes of roving cambots that showed mining tunnels, kilometer after kilometer of deserted tunnel. And finally, many of the screens simply showed the pink-tinged blue of the sky.

"You have come to this place," Euler said loudly, "to help us in our search for correctness, for perfection, for completeness. We are the keys—human and robot—to the synergy of spirit. Synnoetics is our goal. I will introduce the rest of us and we will begin."

"Synnoetics?" Katherine whispered.

"Man and machine," Derec replied, "the whole greater than the sum of the parts."

"It *is* religious!" she rasped. "And how did you know that?"

Derec shrugged. "This all feels so . . . comfortable to me."

"You know Rydberg," Euler said, "and Avernus and Arion." The robots nodded as their names were called. "The rest of us . . . Waldeyer . . ."

"Good day," said a squat, roundish robot with wheels.

"Dante . . ."

"I welcome you," Dante said, his telescopic eyes sticking out several inches from his dome.

"And Wohler."

A magnificent golden machine bowed formally without removing his pincers from his neighbors'. "We are honored," Wohler said.

"We will answer what questions we can from you," Euler said, "and hope that you will do the same."

"If, as you say," Derec told them, "we are all looking for truth and perfection, then our meeting will be fruitful. I would like to begin by asking you why there are certain areas of life here that you will not discuss with us."

Rydberg spoke. "We are in a standby security mode that renders certain information classified by our programming."

"Did our arrival prompt the institution of the security mode?" Katherine asked.

"No," Euler said. "It was in effect when you arrived. If, in fact, you arrived when you said you did. We must ask you again how you came to be here."

Derec decided to try a little truth. It couldn't hurt as long as no mention was made of the Key. Perhaps a dose of the truth might get them to open up about the Key's existence. "We materialized out of thin air atop this very building."

"And where were you before that?" Wohler, the gold one, asked.

Derec walked slowly around the circle, studying his questioners. "A Spacer way station named Rockliffe near Nexon, right on the edge of the Settlement Worlds quarantine zone."

Arion, the mannequin, asked, "What means, then, did you use to get from one place to the other?"

"No means," Derec said. "We were simply transported here."

There was silence for a moment. "This does not coordinate with any information extant in memory," Avernus said, his large dome following Derec's progress around the circle.

"You've found no ship that could have brought us," Derec

said, "and I'm sure you've searched."

"That is correct," Euler said, "and our radar picked up no activity that could have been construed to be a vessel in our atmosphere."

"I can't explain it beyond that," Derec said. "Now, you answer a question for me. Where did you come from?"

"Who are you addressing?" Euler asked.

"All of you," Derec said.

Avernus answered. "All of them except for me were constructed here, on Robot City," he said. "I was . . . awakened here, but believe I was constructed elsewhere."

"Where?"

"I do not know," the large robot replied. "My first i/o memories are of this place. Nothing in my pre-programming suggested anything of an origin."

"Are you trying to say," Katherine broke in, "that all of you know nothing but the company of other robots? That your entire existence is here?"

"Correct," Rydberg said. "Our master programming is well aware of human beings and their societies, but no formal relationship exists between our species."

"Then how did you come to build this place?" Derec asked. "How then, did it become important to you to make a world for humans?"

"We are incomplete without human beings," Waldeyer said, his squat dome swiveling to Derec and then Katherine. "The very laws that govern our existence revolve around human interaction. We exist to serve independent thought, the higher realms of creativity that we are incapable of alone. We discovered this very quickly, without being told. Alone, we simply exist to no end, no purpose. Even artificial intelligence must have a reason to utilize itself. This world is the first utilization of that intelligence. We've been building it for humans, in order to make the perfect atmosphere in which human creativity can flourish to the greater completeness of us all. Without this world we are nothing.

With it, we are vital contributing factors to the ongoing evolution of the universe."

"Why would that matter to you?" Katherine asked.

"I have a theory about that," Dante said, his elongated eyes glowing bright yellow. "We are the product, the child if you will, of higher realms of creative thought. It seems impossible that the drives of that creative thought *wouldn't* permeate every aspect of our programming. We want for nothing. We desire nothing. Yet, the incompleteness of our inactivity makes us . . . feel, for lack of a better word, useless and extraneous. Given the total freedom of our own world, we were driven to function in service."

Derec suddenly felt a terrible sadness well up in him for these unhappy creatures of man's intelligence. "You've done all this, even though you never knew if any people would come here?"

"That is correct," Euler said. "Then David came, and we thought that all would be right. Then came his death, then the calamities, then you . . . suspects to murder. We never meant for anything to be this way."

"When you say calamities," Derec said, "are you speaking of the problems with the storms?"

"Yes," Rydberg said. "The rains threaten our civilization itself, and it's all our own fault. We are breaking apart from the inside out, with nothing to be done about it."

"I don't understand," Derec said.

"We don't expect you to, nor can we tell you why it must be this way," Euler said.

Derec thought about the hot air pumping through the reservoir. "Is the city's rapid growth rate normal?" he asked.

"No," Euler said. "It coincides with David's death."

"Is it because of David's death?"

"We do not know the answer to that," Euler said.

"Wait a moment," Katherine said, walking away from the circle to sit on the floor, her back up against the north wall. "I want to talk to you about our connection with all this . . .

and why Rydberg called this a preliminary trial."

"You were the one who first mentioned the concept of a trial," the robot replied, leaning out of the circle to stare at her. "I only used that term to make you feel comfortable."

"Okay," she said. "I'll play. You say this is a civilization of robots that have never had human interaction, yet obviously someone gave you your initial programming and ability to perform the work on this city."

"Someone . . . yes," Euler said.

"Someone who's in charge," she said.

"No," Euler said. "We are now in group communication with our master programming unit, but it simply provides us with information from which logical decisions are made. Our overall philosophy is service; our means are logical. Other than that, our society has no direction."

"Then why put us on trial at all?" she asked.

"Respect for human life is our First Law," Rydberg said. "When we envisioned our perfect human/robot world, we saw a world in which all shared respect for the First Law. We envisioned a system of humanics that would guide human behavior, just as the Laws of Robotics guide our behavior. Of course, we have been working entirely from theory, but we have made a preliminary list of three laws that would provide the basis for an understanding of humans."

"Cute," Katherine said. "Now they want us to follow the Laws of Robotics."

Derec interrupted her complaint. "Wait. Let's see what they've come up with."

"Thank you, Friend Derec. Our provisional First Law of Humanics is: A human being may not injure another human being, or, through inaction, allow a human being to come to harm."

"Admirable," conceded Derec, "even if it isn't always obeyed. What is your Second Law?"

Rydberg's hesitation before answering gave Derec the

clear impression that the robot wanted to ask a question of its own, but his took precedence under the Second Law of Robotics.

"The Second Law of Humanics is: A human being must give only reasonable orders to a robot and require nothing of it that would needlessly put it into the kind of dilemma that might cause it harm or discomfort."

"Still admirable, but still too altruistic to be always obeyed. And the third?"

"The Third Law of Humanics is: A human being must not harm a robot, or, through inaction, allow a robot to come to harm, unless such harm is needed to keep a human being from harm or to allow a vital order to be carried out."

"Not only is your experience with humans limited, so is your programming," Derec said, shaking his head. "These 'laws' might describe a utopian society of humans and robots, but they certainly don't describe the way humans really behave."

"We have become aware of that," said Rydberg. "Obviously, we are going to have to reconsider our conclusions. Since your arrival we have been subjected to human lies and deceit, concepts beyond our limited understanding."

"But the First Law must stand!" Avernus said loudly, his red photocells glowing brightly. "Human or robot, all are subject to respect for life."

"We certainly aren't arguing that point," Derec said.

"No!" Katherine said, standing angrily and walking back to the circle. "What we're talking about is the lack of respect· with which *we're* being treated here!"

"Kath . . ." Derec began.

"Shut up," Katherine said. "I've been listening to you having wonderful little philosophical conversations with your robot buddies, and I'm getting a little tired of it. Listen, folks. First thing, I demand that you give us access to communications with the outside and that you let us leave. You have no authority to hold us here."

"This is our world," Euler said. "We mean no offense, but all societies are governed by laws, and we fear you have broken our greatest law."

"And what if we have?" she asked. "What happens then?"

"Well," Euler said. "We would do nothing more than keep you from the society of other humans who you could harm."

"Great. So, how do you prove we did anything in order to hold us?"

"Process of elimination," Waldeyer said. "Friend Derec has previously suggested some other possible avenues of explanation, but we feel it is incumbent upon both of you to explore them—not because we are trying to make it difficult for you, but because we respect your creative intelligence more than we respect our own deductive intelligence in an area like this."

Derec watched as Katherine ran hands through her long black hair and took several deep breaths as she tried to get herself together and in a position to work with this. "All right," she said, more calmly. "You said before that you won't let us see the body."

"No," Euler said. "We said that we *can't* let you see the body."

"Why?"

There was silence. Finally Rydberg spoke. "We don't know where it is," he said. "The city began replicating too quickly and we lost it."

"Lost it?" Derec said.

Derec knew it was impossible for a robot to be or look embarrassed, but that was exactly the feeling he was getting from the entire group.

"We really have no idea of where it is," Euler said.

Derec saw an opening and quickly took it. "In order to do this investigation and prove that we're innocent of any First Law transgressions, we *must* have freedom of movement around your city."

"We exist to protect your lives," Euler said. "You've been caught in the rains; you know how dangerous they are. We can't let you out under those conditions."

"Is there advance warning of the rain?" he asked.

"Yes," Rydberg said. "The clouds build in the late afternoon, and the rain comes at night."

"Suppose we promise to not go out when the conditions are unfavorable?" Derec asked.

Wohler, the golden robot, said, "What are human promises worth?"

Katherine pushed her way beneath the hands of the robots to stand in the center of the circle. "What are our lives worth without freedom?"

"Freedom," Wohler echoed.

A dark cloud passed above the skylight, plunging the room into a gray, melancholy halflight, illumination provided by a score of CRT screens, many of them now showing pictures of madly roiling clouds.

The circle broke immediately, the robots, agitated, hurrying toward the door.

"Come," Euler said, motioning to the humans. "The rains are approaching. We must get you back to shelter. There is so much to do."

"What about my suggestion?" Derec called loudly to them.

"Hurry," Euler called, waving his arm as Derec and Katherine walked toward him. "We will think about it and let you know tomorrow."

"And if we can investigate and prove our innocence," Katherine said, "will you then let us contact the outside?"

Euler stood still and fixed her with his photocells. "Let me put it this way," he said. "If you don't prove your innocence, you'll *never* be allowed to contact the outside."

CHAPTER 5
A WITNESS

Derec sat before the CRT screen on the apartment table and watched the "entertainment" that Arion was providing him in the form, at this moment, of sentences and their grammatic diagrams. Before that it had been a compendium of various failed angle trisection theorems, and before that, an incredibly long list of the powers of ten and the various words that had been invented to describe the astronomical numbers those powers represented. It was an insomniac's nightmare.

It was a dark, gray morning, the air heavy with the chill of the night and the rain that had pounded Robot City for many hours. The sky was slate as the remnants of the night's devastation drifted slowly away on the wings of the morning.

He felt like a caged animal, his nerves jangling madly with the notion that he couldn't leave the apartment if he wanted to. They had been dropped off in the early evening after the meeting at the Compass Tower and hadn't seen a supervisor robot since. The CRT had no keyboard and only received whatever data they chose to show him from moment to moment. At this particular time, they apparently felt the need to amuse him; but the time filler of the viewscreen only increased his frustration.

He hadn't slept well. The apartment only had one bed and Katherine was using it. Derec slept on the couch. It had been too short for him, and that didn't make sleeping any easier.

But that wasn't the real reason he'd been awake.

It was the rain.

He couldn't get out of his head the fact that the reservoir had been nearly filled when he'd been flung into it the night before. How, then, could it possibly hold the immense amounts of water that continued to pour into it with each successive rainfall? He'd worried over that point: the more rain, the greater the worry. The fact that the supervisors hadn't contacted him since before the storm seemed ominous. All of their efforts seemed to revolve around the weather problems.

How did the weather tie in with the rapid growth rate of the city? Were the two linked?

"You're up early," came Katherine's voice behind him.

He turned to see her, face soft from sleep, framed by the diffused light. She looked good, a night's sleep bringing out her natural beauty. She was wrapped in the pale green cover from her bed. He wondered idly what she was wearing beneath it, then turned unconsciously to his awakening, after the explosion in Aranimas's ship, in the medical wing of the Rockliffe Station to find her naked on the bed beside. Embarrassed, he pushed that thought aside, but its residue left another thought from that time, something he had completely forgotten about.

"Can I ask you a question?" he said.

Her face darkened and he watched her tighten up. "What is it?" she asked.

"When we were at Rockliffe, Dr. Galen mentioned you had a chronic condition," he said. "Later, when he began to talk about it, you shut him up."

She walked up to look at the screen, refusing to meet his gaze. "You're mistaken," she said. "I'm fine . . . the picture of health."

She turned slightly from him, and there seemed to be a small catch in her voice. When she turned back, her face was set firm, quite unlike the vulnerable morning creature he'd seen a moment ago. "What's happening on the screen?" she asked.

He looked. A pleasant, always changing pattern of computer generated images was juicing through the CRT, accompanied by a random melody bleeped out of the machine's tiny speaker.

"You make it very hard for me to believe you," he said, ignoring the screen. "Why, when we need total honesty and trust between us, do I feel that you're holding back vital information from me?"

"You're just paranoid," she said, and he could tell he was going to get nothing from her. "And if you don't change the subject quickly, I'm going to find myself getting angry, and that's no way to start the day."

He reluctantly agreed. "I'm worried about the rains," he said. "They were worse last night than the night before."

She sat at the table with him. "Well, if this place is getting ready to have major problems, I hope we're out of here before they happen. We've got to get something going with the murder investigation."

"Do you know what makes rain?" he asked, ignoring the issue of the murder.

"What has that got to do with our investigation?" she asked, on edge.

"Nothing," he said. "I'm just wondering about these rains, I . . ."

"Don't say it," she replied holding up a hand. "You're worried about your robot friends. Well, let me tell you something, your friends are in the process of keeping us locked up for the rest of our lives . . ."

"Not locked up, surely," he interrupted.

"This is serious!" she said, angry now. "We have a very good chance of being kept prisoner here for life. You know, once they make a decision like that, I see no reason that they would ever change it. Don't you understand the gravity of the situation?"

He looked at her calmly, placing a hand over hers on the

table. She drew it away, and he felt his own anger rise, then rapidly subside. "I understand the problem," he explained, "but I fear the problem with the city is more pressing, more ... immediate."

"But it's not *our* problem. The murder is."

"Indulge me," he said. "Let's talk about weather for just a minute."

She sighed, shaking her head. "Let's see what I remember," she said. "Molecules respond to heat, separating, moving more quickly. Water molecules are no exception. On a hot day, they rise into the atmosphere and cling to dust particles in the air. When they rise into the cooler atmosphere, they turn into clouds. When the clouds get too heavy, too full of water, they return to the ground in the form of rain."

"Okay," he said. "And wind is simply the interplay of heat and cold in the atmosphere."

She shrugged. "The cold, heavier air pushes down and forces the warm air to move—wind."

"I think I'm beginning to see a connection," he said, excited. "Look. Robot City is building at a furious pace, sending a great deal of dust into the atmosphere." He thought about the reservoir. "Meanwhile, they are somehow liberating a great deal of water from the mining processes that are needed to build the city. Along with the mining processes comes a tremendous amount of kinetic energy, heat, which they are venting into the atmosphere near the water, forcing the heated molecules to rise as water vapor and cling to the dust particles that are thick in the atmosphere right now. At night, the temperature cools down a great deal ..."

"That could be an uncompensated ozone layer," she said.

He pointed to her. "Ozone. That's what seals in our atmosphere. As goes the ozone layer, so go our temperature inversions. So, it cools at night, the rain clouds forming, the cool air bringing on the big winds, and the rain falls."

"So," Katherine said, "if they slowed down the building pace, it could slow down the weather."

"It seems logical to me," he replied.

"So why don't they do it?"

"That's the mystery, isn't it?"

The door slid open and Wohler, the golden robot, moved into the room, flanked on either side by smaller robots.

"Good morning," Wohler said. "I trust your sleep-time was beneficial."

"You're going to have to learn to knock before you come barging in here," Katherine said. "Now go out and do it again."

Derec watched the robot dutifully march outside the door and slide it closed. He knew that Katherine was simply venting frustration. On Spacer worlds, robots were considered simply part of the furniture and their presence was not thought about in terms of privacy.

There was a gentle tapping on the door, the nature of the material muffling the sound somewhat.

"Come in," Katherine said with satisfaction, and the door slid open, the robots reentering.

"Is this the preferred method of treatment in future?" Wohler asked.

"It is," she replied.

"Very well," the robot said, then noticed Derec's sleeping covers on the sofa. "Should these be returned to the bedroom?"

"You only provided us with one bed," Derec replied. "I slept out here."

Wohler moved farther into the room, coming up near the table. "Did we err? Was the sleeping space too small . . ."

"Katherine and I would simply like . . . separate places to sleep," Derec said.

"Privacy?" Wohler asked. "As with the knocking on the door?"

"Yes," Katherine said, and he could tell she was unwilling to delve into the social aspects of human sleeping arrangements, so he left it alone, too.

"On-line time is a matter of priorities right now," the robot said, "but we will see if we can arrange something for you that is more private."

"Thanks," Derec said. "And if it takes another day to arrange it, that's all right with me. It's Katherine's turn to sleep on the couch tonight."

"What?" she said loudly. Derec grinned broadly at her. She wasn't amused.

He quickly changed the subject. "What brings you here this morning, Wohler?" he asked. "Have you reached a decision about our requests of yesterday?"

"Yes," the robot replied. "And it is our sincerest wish that the decision be one that all of us can accept. First, in addressing the issue of your investigation and freedom of movement. We conferred at as great a length as time would permit under the present circumstances, and decided that, despite your flaws, you *are* human, and that fact in and of itself demands that we give you the benefit of the doubt in this situation. Many of our number were concerned about your veracity, or lack of it, but I reminded them that a great *human* philosopher once said, 'Isn't it better to have men being ungrateful than to miss a chance to do good?' And so my fellows voted to do good in this regard."

"Excellent," Derec said.

"But . . ." Katherine helped.

"Indeed," Wohler returned. "It is my place to philosophize in any given situation, and I need remind you now that one must always be prepared to take bad along with good."

"Just get on with it," Katherine said.

Wohler nodded. "On the matter of your safety, and your . . . unpredictability, it was decided that each of you would have a robot companion to . . . help you in your investigations."

"You mean to guard us," Katherine said.

"Merely a matter of semantics," Wohler countered, and Derec could tell that the robot had been geared for diplomacy. "Actually, in this case, I believe you may find these robots more useful as assistants than as protection. In fact, one of them was present during the death of David and the subsequent confusion."

Katherine perked up. "Really? Which one?"

The robot to Wohler's left came forward. Its body was tubular, its dome a series of bristling sensors and photocells. Without arms, it seemed useless in almost any sense.

"What are you called?" Katherine asked the machine.

The machine's tones were clipped and precise. "I am Event Recorder B-23, Model 13 Alpha 4."

"I'll call you Eve, if that's all right," Katherine said, standing and wrapping her blanket a little tighter around herself. She looked at Derec. "I want this one."

"Fine," Derec said, then to the other, "come here."

The robot moved up close to him. "You'll answer to Rec."

"Rec," the robot repeated.

"We call these robots witnesses," Wohler said. "Their only function is to witness events precisely for later reporting."

"That's why they have no arms," Derec said.

"Correct," Wohler replied. "They are unequipped to do anything but witness. Once involvement begins on any level, the witness function falters in any creature. These robots only witness and report. They will know the how of almost everything, but never the why. They will answer all of your questions to the best of their ability, but again, they are unable to make any second-level connections by putting events together to form reasons."

"I'm going to go get dressed," Katherine said, the happiest Derec had seen her in days. She hurried out of the room, disappearing down the hall to the bedroom.

"Where will we be denied access?" Derec asked. "Or is the entire planet open to us?"

"Alas, no," Wohler said. "You will be denied access to certain parts of the city and certain operations. Your witness, however, will tell you when you've stepped into dangerous water, as it were."

"What are the chances of me getting around a terminal,"

Derec asked, "and talking to the central core?"

"The central core has sealed itself off because of our present state of emergency," Wohler said. "It will not accept input from any sources save the supervisors, and we are unable to help you in this regard."

"How do the day-to-day operations survive?" he asked.

"Essential information can be gathered through any terminal," the robot answered. "But input is limited."

"You don't mind if I try?"

"That is between you and the central core. We all have our jobs to do. All that we insist upon is that you honor your commitment to come back here when the rains approach. We must put your safety above all else. Having failed in this regard with your predecessor, we perhaps err on the side of caution. But all privileges will be denied should this directive be overlooked or ignored."

"I understand," Derec replied, "and will respect your wishes."

"Your words, unfortunately, mean very little right now," the robot said, turning to the door, his head swiveling back to Derec. "By your deeds we will judge you in future. As an Earth philosopher once said, 'The quality of a life is determined by its activities.' Now, I must go."

With that, Wohler moved quickly through the opening and departed hurriedly down the elevator. The activity bothered Derec; it said to him that things were not going well in Robot City. He had intended to ask Wohler about the effects of last night's rain, but then decided a first-hand look might be better and determined that Rec would take him where he wanted to go.

"There," Katherine said, coming down the hall to bustle around the room. She wore a blue one-piece that the dinner servo-robot had brought with it the night before. "Finally, we can start moving in a positive direction. Where do you want to start?"

"I thought I'd go down to the reservoir," he replied, "and see how much rain fell last night."

She stopped walking and stared, unbelieving, at him. "Don't you realize that every moment is precious right now? We need to find that body and see what happened. It could be . . . decomposing or something at this very minute."

"I've got to see if there was any damage," he said. "I'll try and join you later."

"Never mind," she said angrily, and walked quickly to the door. "Satisfy your stupid urges. I don't *want* you with me. You'll just get in the way anyhow. Come on, Eve. We've got a *corpus delecti* to find."

She walked out of the apartment without a backward glance and was gone, Derec frowning after her. He couldn't help the way his feelings ran on this. He felt that so much of his own life, his own reasons for being, hinged upon the future of Robot City that its troubles seemed to be his own.

"I want to go to the reservoir," he told Rec. "Can you take me there?"

"Yes, Friend Derec," the robot answered, and they left together.

When they arrived at street level, Derec was disappointed to find that the supervisors hadn't left any transportation for him to use. A great deal of time would be wasted walking from place to place. Perhaps he could talk to Euler about it later, though he feared that the reasons had much to do with keeping him from going very far from home.

"Do you want to go the most direct route?" the witness asked him.

"Yes, of course," Derec said as they set out walking. "Let me ask you a question. Is the rain a result of the work being done on the city?"

"For the most part," Rec answered through a speaker located on Derec's side of his dome. "It is also the rainy season here."

"If they slowed down the building, would it slow down the rain?"

"I do not know."

Derec was going about this wrong, asking the wrong

questions of a witness. "How does the city make rain?" he asked.

The robot began talking, recalling information in an encyclopedic fashion. "Olivine is mined below ground and crushed in vacuum, releasing carbon, hydrogen, oxygen, and nitrogen, from which water vapor, carbon dioxide, methane gas, and traces of other chemicals are liberated. Iron ore is also being mined for building materials, along with petroleum products for plastics . . ."

"Plastics?" Derec asked.

"Plastics are used as alloys in making the material from which the city is constructed. Do you wish me to go on with my previous line of witnessing?"

"Let me tell you," Derec said, "and you tell me if I'm right. Water vapor, along with the heat energy from the mining process, is pumped into the air, heat also being pumped into the reservoir. The CO_2 is bled into the forest to help growth. The reason that the weather is so rainy now is that the city is growing too fast, giving off too much heat, dust, and water."

"I do not know why the weather is *so* rainy right now," Rec said. "I do not even understand what *so* rainy means. The other statements you made are juxtapositional with statements I heard Supervisor Avernus make, which I assume to be correct."

"Fine," Derec said. "Is there a problem with the ozone layer?"

"Problem?" the robot asked.

Derec rephrased. "Is any work being done on the ozone layer?"

"I do not know," Rec said, "although I did hear Supervisor Avernus say on one occasion that the 'ozone layer needs to be increased photochemically to ten parts per million.'"

"Good," Derec said. "Very good."

"You are pleased with my witnessing?" Rec asked.

"Yes," Derec replied. "Will the supervisors be asking you to witness later what we've discussed?"

"That is my function, Friend Derec."

They walked for nearly an hour by Derec's watch, the city still subtly changing around them. It sometimes took a while to get information out of the witness, but if questions were phrased properly, Derec found Rec an endless source of information, and he wondered how Katherine was faring with her witness.

Derec knew they were nearing the reservoir long before they arrived there. A long stream of robots was moving toward and away from the site, followed by large vehicles bearing slabs of city building material.

They walked into an area sonorous with activity, echoes raising the pitch enough that Derec covered his ears against the din. Within the confines of the reservoir area, his worst fears were realized. The water had reached the top of the pool and was splashing over slightly in various areas.

For their part, the robots were doing their best to stop it. Large machines, obviously converted from mining work, had been modified to lift huge slabs of the building material to the top of the pool, where utility robots with laser torches were welding the higher sections together, trying for more room, bathing the area in various sections in showers of yellow sparks.

It was a massive job, the reservoir covering many acres, as the robots worked frantically to finish before the next rain. And to Derec's mind, this could be no more than a stopgap measure, for unless the rain was halted, it would overflow even the extra section in a day or two.

"What happens if the water overflows?" he asked Rec.

"I am unable to speculate on such matters, Friend Derec," the robot said. "It is not overflowing. When it does, I will witness."

"Right," Derec said, and moved forward, closing on the workers.

"Do not get too close," Rec called. "It is dangerous for you."

Derec ignored him and moved closer, recognizing Euler,

who was helping with the movement of a slab. He was directing a large, heavy-based machine with a telescoping arm that held a six-by-six-meter slab in magnetic grips. He was holding his pincers at the approximate distance the arm had yet to travel so that it would be flush with the edge of the pool and the slab next to it. Utility robots physically guided the slabs to the ground and held them so the welders could set to work immediately.

"Euler!" Derec called, the robot jerking to the sound of his name.

"It is too dangerous for you here!" Euler called back, waving him away. "We have no safety controls over this area!"

"I'll only stay a centad," Derec said, moving up close to him. He could look past the end of the last slab and see the dark waters churning the top of the pool. In the distance, all around the reservoir, he could see the same operation being repeated by other crews.

"What are you doing here?" Euler asked him.

"I had to see for myself," Derec answered. "I knew the levels were rising. Why don't you stop the building pace and let these waters recede?"

"I can't tell you why," Euler said.

"But what happens when this overflows?"

"We lose the treatment plant," Euler said, holding his pincers up to signify to the arm to stop moving the slab. Then he motioned toward the ground, the arm bringing the slab down very slowly. "We lose much of our mining operations. We lose a great many miners. We will have failed."

"Then stop the building!"

"We can't!"

Just then, a utility robot working the slab was bumped slightly by the moving metal and lost its footing on the wet floor. Soundlessly and without drama, it slipped from the edge of the pool and fell into the dark waters, disappearing immediately.

Everything stopped.

Euler pushed past Derec to hurry to the water's edge, where he stood, head down, watching. The rest of the crew did the same, lining up quietly beside the water. Derec moved to join Euler.

"I'm sorry," he said.

Euler slowly turned his head to look at the boy, not saying anything for a long time. "I should have paid more attention," he said.

"How deep is the water?" Derec asked.

"Very deep," Euler replied. "I was talking with you and didn't give the job my complete attention."

"Can it be saved?"

"Had there been more time," Euler said, "the job would have been studied for safety and feasibility and this wouldn't have happened. Had I known better, I wouldn't have allowed you to come so close. A robot is lost, and the supervisor is to blame."

"There was nothing you could have done," Derec said.

"A robot is dead today," Euler told him. "I will not answer any more of your questions right now."

"If the city keeps moving," Katherine asked, "how can you take me to the location of the murder?"

"Triangulation," Eve, the witness, said. "Using the Compass Tower as one point and the exact position of the sun at a given time as another point, my sensors are able to triangulate the position where I first witnessed the body. The time is the only real factor at this point. We must gauge the sun in exactly 13.24 decads to get the position right."

They were walking through the city, Katherine feeling a mixture of fear and exuberance at her first solo trip outside. They were walking high up, above many of the buildings, bridges between structures seemingly growing for her to walk across, then melting away after her passage. Eve apparently needed the height in order to take the precise measurements.

Katherine was angry at Derec for his lack of interest in their predicament, but she knew him well enough to know how stubborn he could be. She, in fact, knew him far better than he knew himself, and that was maddening. They were caught in a web of intrigue that existed on a massive level, and as long as she was trapped there, she had to play the situation with as much control as she could muster. And that included not telling Derec any more about his life than he could figure out for himself. Her own existence was at stake, and until she could escape the maze that had locked up their activities, she desperately feared saying anything more.

She *had* to get away from Robot City. The pain had increased since her arrival here, and, for the first time in her life, death was a topic she found herself dwelling upon.

And her only crime was love.

She felt the tears begin to well up and fought them back with an iron will. They wouldn't help her here. Nothing would, except her own tenacity and intelligence.

"Tell me about your involvement in David's death," she asked Eve, who was busy calibrating against the sun.

"In approximately two decads," the robot said, "it will have happened exactly nine days ago. We go down from here."

Eve moved directly to the corner of the six-story structure they were standing upon, and railed stairs formed for them to walk down. As they descended, the robot continued talking.

"I was called upon to witness the attempts to free Friend David from an enclosed room."

"An enclosed room?" Katherine said. "I've never heard about this. How could he get trapped like that in this place?"

"The room grew around him." Eve said. They reached street level and the robot headed west, away from the Compass Tower. "It sealed him in and wouldn't let him leave."

"Why?"

"I do not know."

"Does anyone know?"

"I do not know."

"All right," Katherine said, watching a team of robots carry what looked to be gymnasium equipment into one of the buildings. "Just report what you saw."

"Gladly. I was called upon to witness the attempt to free Friend David from the sealed room. When I arrived, Supervisor Dante was already on the scene . . ." The robot stopped moving and for several seconds stared up into the sun. "Precisely here." Eve pointed to a section of the street. "Friend David was caught inside the structure and we could hear him shouting to be let out."

"Who?"

"Myself, Supervisor Dante, a utility robot with a torch, and another household utility robot who first discovered Friend David's problem."

"What happened then?"

"Then Supervisor Dante asked Utility Robot #237-5 if the laser torch was safe to use in such close proximity to a human being, and Utility Robot #237-5 assured him that it was. At that point, Supervisor Dante tried to reason with the room to release Friend David, and failing that, he requested that the room be cut into with the torch."

"And that request was complied with?"

"Yes. Supervisor Dante, in fact, asked Utility Robot #237-5 to complete the project quickly."

"Why?"

"I do not know."

Katherine thought about the nature of the witness and asked another question. "Were there any other events that coincided with this event?"

"Yes," Eve said. "Food Services complained that Friend David could not be served lunch on time and inquired if that would be dangerous to his health; several of the supervisors were meeting in the Compass Tower to discuss ways in which Friend David might have come to the city without their knowledge; and the city itself was put on general security alert."

"Does a general security alert alter the way in which functions are performed?" she asked.

"Yes. We were all called to other emergency duties, and were here only because of the danger to Friend David and the need to release him."

"Which you did."

"Not me," Eve said. "I only witnessed. But Friend David was freed from the enclosed room."

"Did you notice anything odd at that point?"

"Odd? Friend Katherine, I can only . . ."

"I know," she interrupted, a touch frustrated. "You only witness. Then tell me exactly what happened."

"Supervisor Dante asked Friend David to return to his apartment because a security alert had been called. Friend David said that he was not ready to return to his apartment, that he had business to do. Then he complained of a headache. Then he started laughing and walked away. Utility Robot #237-5 then asked Supervisor Dante if Friend David should be apprehended, and Supervisor Dante said he had weighed the priorities and had decided that the security alert took precedence and ordered us to proceed to our emergency duties, which, in my case, involved witnessing something that I am not at liberty to discuss with you."

"Then what?" Katherine asked, anxious.

"Then I performed the security duty that I had been assigned."

"No, no," Katherine said. "What happened then in regard to David?"

"Approximately nine decads later, I was again called upon." Eve began moving quickly down the street, Katherine right behind, having to run to keep up. "I am taking you to the approximate place of the second incident," the robot called from a speaker set in the back of its dome. "I was called here, along with Supervisor Euler this time, by Utility Robot #716-14, who had discovered several waste control robots trying to take the body of Friend David away."

Eve moved quickly around a corner, then stopped abruptly, Katherine nearly running into the robot.

"Here," Eve said, "is the approximate place where the body was alleged to have fallen."

"Alleged?"

"It was no longer here upon my arrival."

"What story did the utility robot tell?"

"Utility Robot #716-14 said that he sent the waste control robots away, then examined Friend David for signs of life without success. During the course of the examination another room began to grow around the body and enclose it, at which point Utility Robot #716-14 removed himself before becoming trapped, and put in an emergency call to us. We returned to the scene together, but the body was gone. That is the last time anyone has seen Friend David."

"Were there signs of violence on the body?"

"Utility Robot #716-14 reported that the body appeared perfectly normal except for a small cut on the left foot. Since I can only report hearsay in this regard, I am unable to render this as an accurate examination."

Katherine leaned against the wall of a one-story parts depot, the wall giving slightly under her pressure. It seemed more than coincidence that David's plight in the sealed room and the alert conditions of the city happened concurrently— but how were they connected?

"Do you feel, then, that the body moved simply because the city moved it?" she asked.

"I cannot speculate on such a theory," the witness said, "but I heard Supervisor Euler make a pronouncement similar to yours—hearsay again."

"Given the growth rate of the city," Katherine said, "calculate how far and in what direction the body of David could have traveled if, indeed, the movement of the city took him from this place."

"Approximately ten and one-half blocks," Eve said without hesitation, "in *any* direction. The city works according to a plan that is not known to me."

"Ten and a half blocks," Katherine said low. "Well, it'll sure give me something to do to fill in the time." She looked at Eve's bristling dome. "Let's take a walk."

"That is your decision," the robot replied, as Katherine picked a direction at random and began walking, looking for what, she didn't know.

ACCESS DENIED was written in bold letters across the CRT, and it was a phrase Derec had run into over a dozen times in as many minutes.

He stood at a small counter set beside a large, open window. Through the billowing clouds of iron-red dust floating into the sky, he could see the long line of earthmovers inching their way along the rocky ground, the teeth of their heavy front diggers easily chewing up the ground to a depth of 70 centimeters, then laying out the mulch in a flat, even plain behind, holes filling, rises falling, the ground absolutely uniform behind. A series of heavy rollers completed the unique vehicles, packing the ground hard for the slab base of the city to push its way into that section as it was completed.

After leaving the reservoir and its tragedy behind, he had asked Rec to take him to the edge of the city. He had wanted to see for himself the creation of the cloud dust and also to try and find access to a terminal far out of the reach of the supervisors. The robot had been hesitant at first, but after Derec had assured him that he'd go no farther than city's edge, Rec had readily agreed.

But now that he was here, Derec resented the time it had taken to come this far out. The terminal had been a complete bust. He'd found himself able to access any amount of information when it came to this part of the city operation: troubleshooting info, repair info, time references, equipment specs, personnel delineation, and SOPs of all kinds; but beyond that, access was impossible.

He had tried various methods of obtaining passwords, but it seemed he was stymied before he got started. He came away with the impression that once the city was on alert, terminals became place-oriented, only able to pick up specific data as it related to their possible function in a given location. He found this difficult to believe, for if the robots were in total charge of access and passwords it belied the nature of their "perfect human world." It struck him that access would have to be humanly possible for very basic philosophical reasons.

But not here; not at this terminal.

So, where did that leave him? The rains still came, with or without his presence; the central core was still denied to him, and with it any answers it might possess; he was still a prisoner (a fact he *did* take seriously, despite Katherine's feelings); and he still knew nothing about his origins or reasons for being in Robot City.

That thought returned him to the basics. When he had visited the Compass Tower, Avernus had been pointed out as the first supervisor robot, the one that had initiated the construction of the other supervisors. Derec had been successful in determining the origin and destination of the water; now he would work on the origin of the city itself. The only place to start was with Avernus and the underground. The mining was needed to produce the raw materials to build the city. Everything else sprang from that foundation. He would go to the source—to Avernus.

He shut down the useless terminal and walked out of the otherwise bare room to find Rec intently studying the rising dust clouds, taking readings. It was his obsession.

"I want to go into the mines and speak with Avernus," he told the robot. "Is that acceptable?"

"I will take you to the mines, Friend Derec," Rec answered, "but from that point on, the decision will belong to Avernus."

"Fair enough," Derec said, and prepared for another long walk. Then he spotted one of the trams parked near the excavation and walked toward it. "Let's ride this time."

"We were not given this machine," Rec said. "It is not ours to take."

"Were you told *not* to let me take the machine?" Derec countered.

"No, but . . ."

"Then let's go."

Derec jumped in the front, but saw no controls with which to drive it. He knew that this was probably the means by which the robots working the movers got here, but the witness was unable to make that speculation and consequently folded up. "How does it work?"

"You speak your destination into the microphone," Rec said.

"The underground," Derec said, then shrugged at Rec.

Within seconds, the car lurched forward and moved speedily away from the digs.

They traveled quickly, moving through an entire section full of nothing but robot production facilities that were running full tilt, furiously trying to keep up with the record-setting building pace. As the number of buildings increased, so, too, did the number of robots to service those buildings and the people who didn't live in them. They passed vehicle after vehicle jammed full of new, functionally designed robots who stared all around, seeing their world for the first time.

They also passed other small forests and what seemed to be large sections of hydroponic greenhouses, for when large-scale food production became a reality. Then they whizzed past a large, open area that seemed to serve no function.

"What's that?" Derec asked.

"Nothing," Rec answered.

"I don't mean now," Derec said. "What's it going to be?"

"I do not often deal in potential," the robot replied, several red lights on his dome blinking madly, "but I recall Supervisor Euler once referring to this place as a future spaceport."

Derec was a bit taken aback. Robot City was absolutely unable to deal with incoming or outgoing ships in any form. It led him down another avenue.

"If the spaceport hasn't been constructed yet," he said, "where do you keep your hyperwave transmitters?"

He asked the question casually, knowing full well that Rec would undoubtedly tell him the information was classified; but he was totally unprepared for the answer he received.

"I do not know what a hyperwave transmitter is," the robot replied.

"A device designed for communication over long distances in space," Derec said. "Perhaps you call it something else."

"I have witnessed nothing designed to communicate beyond our atmosphere," Rec answered.

"You don't send and receive information from off-planet?"

"I know of no such instance," Rec replied. "We are self-contained here."

The tram jerked to a stop, jerking Derec's thoughts along with it. Somehow, it had never occurred to him that they really were trapped on this planet. The Key and its proper use suddenly became of paramount importance to him.

"We have arrived, Friend Derec," Rec said.

"So we have," Derec replied, getting slowly out of the car. What was going on here? Who created this place? And why? It was a pristine civilization removed from contact with anything beyond itself, yet its Spacer roots were obvious. Could David, the dead man, have been the creator?

He walked past the lines of robots carrying their damaged equipment, past the huge extruder and its never-ending ribbon of city, and stood at the entrance to the underground. He turned to see Rec standing beside him.

"Find Avernus," he said. "Tell him I want to speak with him. I don't want to break protocol by going somewhere off-limits to humans."

"Yes, Friend Derec," the robot answered and moved aside to commune with its net of radio communications.

Derec sat on the ground beside the doorway and watched the robots walking back and forth past him. He was beginning to feel like a useless appendage with nothing to do. He felt guilty even ordering the robots around; they had more important things to do.

He glanced at his watch. It was two in the afternoon, and soon they'd be approaching another night of rain, another useless night of speculation as the water level rose higher and higher. "We will have failed," Euler had said, and in that sentence the robot had spoken volumes. Like Derec, the supervisor knew that Robot City was a test, a test designed for all of then. If Euler and the others were unable to solve the problem of the rain, they would have failed in their attempt to build a workable world. He also knew that the salvation of this world would take a creative form of thought that most people felt robots incapable of. Perhaps that's where Derec fit in. Synnoetics, they had called it, the whole greater than the sum of the parts. For that to take place, Derec would have to begin by convincing the robots they had to confide in him despite their security measures.

"I'm extremely busy, Friend Derec," the voice said loudly. "What do you want of me?"

Derec looked up to see Avernus's massive form bending to fit in the door space.

"We need to speak of saving this place," Derec said. "We need to approach one another as equals, and not adversaries."

"You may have done murder, Derec," Avernus said. "I am not the equal of that."

"Neither is Euler," Derec replied, "but his inattention caused a robot to die today."

"You were also present."

Derec looked at the ground. "Y-yes," he said. "I had no right to bring that up."

"Tell me what you want of me."

"Answers," Derec said. "Understanding. I want to help with the city . . . the rains. I want someone to know and appreciate that."

The robot looked at him for a long moment, then motioned him inside. They walked down the stairs together and into the holding area, Rec following behind at a respectable distance. Avernus then took him aside, away from the activity, and made a seat for him by piling up a number of broken machines of various kinds.

Derec climbed atop the junk pile and sat, Avernus standing nearby. "We are in an emergency situation, and my programming limits my communication with you."

"I understand that," Derec replied. "I also know that many situations require judgment calls that you must sift through your logic circuits. I ask only that you think synnoetically."

"If you ask that of me," the robot said, "I must tell you something. The concept of death holds more weight with me than with the others. My logic circuits are different because of my work."

"I don't understand."

"The robot's stock-in-trade is efficiency," Avernus answered, "and in jobs requiring labor, cost efficiency. But in the mines cost efficiency isn't necessarily cost efficient."

"Now I'm really confused."

"The most cost-effective way to approach mine work may be the most dangerous way to approach it, but the most dangerous way to approach it may result in the loss of a great many workers because of the nature of the mines. So, the most effective way to work the mines may not be the most cost-efficient in the long run. Consequently, I am programmed to have a respect for life—even robotic life—that far and away exceeds what one could consider normal. The lives of my workers are of prime importance to me beyond any concept of efficiency."

"What has that got to do with me?" Derec asked.

"If you have killed, Derec, you will be anathema to me. The fact that you are accused and could be capable of such an action is almost more than I can bear. I voted against your freedom when we met on this issue."

"I swear to you that I am innocent," Derec said.

"Humans lie," the robot answered. "Now, do you still wish me to be the one to 'appreciate' your position?"

"Yes," Derec answered firmly. "I ask only that I be given the opportunity to show you that I have the best interests of Robot City at heart. I am innocent, and the truth will free me."

"Well said. What do you want to know?"

"You are the first supervisor," Derec said. "What are your first recollections?"

"I was awakened by a utility robot we call l-l," Avernus said, his red photocells fixed on Derec. "l-l had already awakened fifty other utility machines. I awakened with a full knowledge of who and what I was: a semi-autonomous robot whose function was to supervise the mines for city building, and to supervise the building of other supervisors to fulfill various tasks."

"Were you programmed to serve humans?"

"No," Avernus said quickly. "We were programmed with human information, both within us and within the core unit, which was also operational when I was awakened. Our decision to service was one we arrived at independently."

"Could that be the reason that the robots here have been less than enthusiastic about Katherine and me?" Derec asked. "Not knowing human reality, you accepted an ideal that was impossible for us to live up to."

"That is, perhaps, true," Avernus agreed.

"How long ago did your awakening take place?"

"A year ago, give or take."

"And did you see any human beings, or have knowledge of any, at that time?"

"No. Our first action was the construction of the Compass Tower. After that, we began our philosophical deliberations as to our purpose in the universe."

"How about l-l? Did he have any contact with humans?"

"It never occurred to us to ask," Avernus said.

"Where is l-l now?" Derec asked, feeling himself working toward something.

"In the tunnels," Avernus said, gesturing toward the elevators. "l-l works the mines."

Derec jumped off the makeshift seat. "Take me there," he said.

"Security. . ." the robot began.

"I'm a human being," Derec said. "This world was designed for me and my kind. I'm sorry, Avernus, but if you exist to serve, it's time you started to act like it. If you respect your own philosophies, you must accept the fact that your security measures were not designed to keep you secure from human beings. If they were, there is something desperately wrong with your basic philosophy."

"It is dangerous in the mines," Avernus replied.

"You can protect me."

The robot stood looking between Derec and the elevator doors. "I must deny you the central core," he said at length. "I must deny you knowledge of our emergency measures. But you are a human being, and this is your world to share with us. I will take you to l-l and protect you. If, at some point, protecting you means sending you back to the surface, I will do that."

"Fair enough," Derec said, looking at his watch. "We must go."

They moved toward the elevators, Rec joining them within the large car. In deference to the supervisor, the other robots let them have the car to themselves. Avernus pushed a stud in the wall and the door closed. The car started downward.

It went down a long way.

"The trick to movement in the mines is deliberation," Avernus said, as the car shuddered to a stop.

"Deliberation," Derec repeated.

The door slid open to delirious activity. Thousands of utility robots moved through a huge cavern that stretched as far as Derec could see in either direction. A continuous line of train cars rolled past on movable tracks, delivering raw ore to the giant smelters that refined it to more workable stages where it was heated and alloyed with other materials. The ceiling was thirty-five meters high and cut from the raw earth. Clean rooms filled the space at regular intervals.

"Iron!" Avernus said, stretching his arms wide. "The foundation upon which the ferrous metals are based, from which the modern world is made possible. We mine it in huge quantities, using it in its raw state to make our equipment, and alloyed with special plastics to form our city. There!"

He pointed to a machine through which layers of iron were belt-feeding, together with imprinted patterns of micro-circuits. The congealed mass issued from the top of the machine and proceeded through the ceiling in a continuous ribbon, the building material that Derec had seen extruded on the surface.

"That is the stuff of Robot City," Avernus said. "Iron and plastic alloy, cut with large amounts of carbon, and using carbon monoxide as a reducing agent. The 'skin' is then imprinted with millions of micro-circuits per square meter. In centimeter, independent sections, the 'skin' is alive with robotic intelligence, geared to human needs and protection. The whole is pre-programmed to build and behave in a pre-scribed fashion, and to react to human needs as they arise."

"That's why the walls give when I push on them," Derec said, moving gingerly out of the elevator and staying close to Avernus.

"Exactly. Now remember, deliberation. Stay close."

Avernus moved out into the middle of the furious activity, machines and robots and train cars rushing quickly all around them. As Avernus stepped into the path of on-rushing vehicles, Derec froze, wanting to pull back. But the expected accidents never took place, the robots and their machines gauging all the actions around them and reacting perfectly to them.

That's when the concept of deliberation became clear to Derec. Movement needed to be deliberate, with constant forward momentum. All judgment was based on the idea that movement would be steady and could be avoided once gauged. It was the erratic movement that was dangerous—the abrupt stop, the jump back; down here, such movements would be fatal.

Once he understood the concept, it became easier to walk

into the path of on-rushing vehicles. And as they moved through the center of the great hall, Derec began to feel more comfortable.

"Let me ask you a question," he said to the big robot. "Did you invent the 'skin' of Robot City?"

"No," Avernus replied. "Its program was already within the central core."

"So its activities are all pre-programmed?"

"Correct. All we did was use it once we decided to be of service to humanity."

They reached an edge of the hall, dozens of smaller tunnels branching off from it.

"We ride now," Avernus said, climbing into a cart that was far too small for his immense bulk. Derec and Rec climbed in with him, and Avernus started off right away, taking them down a barely lit tunnel.

"This one looks deserted," Derec said, and they hurried along at a fast clip.

"It was, until two days ago," Avernus said. "It is now, perhaps, going to save us."

"How?"

"You will see."

They rode for several more minutes through the dark, going deeper into the earth. Then Derec heard activity ahead.

"We are approaching," Avernus said.

"Approaching what?" Derec asked.

Avernus turned a corner and they were suddenly confronted by a widening of the tunnel, several hundred robots working furiously within an ever-growing space, scooping out dirt into any available container or skid, anything that would move earth. They then would take the earth and move quickly with it down adjoining tunnels, refilling that which had been excavated sometime previously. Like an ant farm, they moved in graceful cooperation and determination, and standing atop a cart, looming above them, was Rydberg, silently pointing as he transmitted his orders by radio to the toiling robots.

Avernus turned and looked at Derec. "Somewhere in there," he said, "you will find l-l."

Katherine's first thought had been that it was a monument, but then she realized there were no monuments on Robot City. It was set on a narrow pedestal about one hundred feet in the air. Located in the middle of a block, the city had simply built itself around the object in a semicircle, leaving it set apart from all other structures by a gap of fifty feet. She had spent several hours walking the changing topography of Robot City without success, but she stopped the moment she came upon this place. If she wanted to compare the workings of the living city to a human body, this room atop the pedestal was like a wound, sealing itself off with scar tissue to protect it from the vital workings of the rest of the body.

It was no more than a room. Katherine stood at ground level staring up at the thing. A box, perhaps five meters square, totally enclosed. The robots took the workings of their city for granted and simply accepted this anomaly. To the creative eye, it stuck out like a solar eclipse on a bright afternoon.

Katherine continued to stare up at it because she didn't want to lose it. Even now, the city continued to move, to grow before her eyes, and as the buildings turned in their slow waltz of life, she turned with them, always keeping the room within her vision. Eve, meanwhile, was trying to round up a supervisor who could effect a means of getting inside the structure and checking it out.

During the course of this excursion, Katherine had begun

to develop a grudging respect for the workings of the city. Obviously, things were not going well right now, but in the long run such a system could be quite beneficial to the humans and robots who inhabited it. The safety factor alone made the system worthwhile. Derec's harrowing ride down through the aqueduct resulted in nothing more than fatigue and a few bruises, all because the system itself was trying to protect him. To Katherine's mind, such a journey on Aurora would have caused Derec's death. She smiled at the thought of a Derec-proof city.

She'd also had time, while waiting for Eve to reach a supervisor, to notice the changes taking place around her. She felt as if she were visiting a resort at the tail end of the off season, all the seasonal workers arriving and getting the place shipshape for the influx of visitors. Clocks were being installed in various parts of the city, and street signs were beginning to go up. The largest change taking place, however, was the increased production and distribution of chairs. Robots had no need for sitting or reclining, and chairs were at a premium; but as they tried to make their city as welcome as possible for humans, they worked diligently to do things just right, despite the fact that the city's emergency measures were forcing many of them into extra duty. She wondered if she'd be this gracious if it were her city. The thought humbled her a bit.

Despite the differences, despite the bind the robots had put them in, they really were trying to make this world as perfect as they could for the travelers, travelers whom they suspected of murder. She had never before considered just how symbiotic the binding of humans to robots really was and, at least for the robots, how essential. She hoped that they would, eventually, have their civilization, complete with humans to order them around stupidly. She found herself smiling again. Her mother had a phrase that could apply to the robots' longing for human companionship—a glutton for punishment.

She heard a noise behind her and turned, expecting to see

a supervisor arriving. Instead she saw two utility robots moving toward her, carrying between them what looked for all the world like a park bench. Without a word, they moved right up to her and placed the bench just behind. She sat, and they hurried off.

She sat for barely a decad before Arion came clanking around a corner, along with a utility robot with a bulky laser torch strapped on his back. It took her back for a second, a seeming replay of the scene Eve had described to her when David had first become trapped in the sealed room.

"Good afternoon, Friend Katherine," Arion said as he moved up to her. "I see you are taking advantage of one of our chairs to rest your body. Very good."

"What's that on your wrist," Katherine asked, "a watch?"

The supervisor held up his arm, displaying the timepiece. "A show of solidarity," he said.

"You're in charge of human-creative functions on Robot City, aren't you?" she asked.

"Human-creative is a redundant term," Arion replied. "Creativity is the human stock-in-trade. I hope you've found satisfactory the entertainments I've provided for you."

"We'll talk about that later," she answered.

"Of course."

"I thank you for coming so promptly," Katherine said.

"This is a priority matter," the robot said, gazing up at the sealed room. "You believe this to be the location of the body?"

"I'm certain of it."

"Very good. Let's take a closer look."

Katherine stood and walked to the base of the tower with Arion. The pedestal was approximately the size of a large tree trunk, just large enough that she could almost reach around it if she tired. Arion reached out and touched the smooth, blue skin, and magically a spiral staircase with railing jutted from the surface and wound around the exterior of the tower.

"After you," the robot said politely.

Katherine started up, the design of the staircase keeping her from any sense of vertigo. As she climbed, she could feel that the air was cooling down, the presage to another night of destructive rain. Behind her, Arion, the utility robot, and the witness followed dutifully, and she realized that she was in the lead because it was the natural position for her in regard to this inquiry. This was her notion, her case—the robots at this point were merely her willing co-horts. Finally, she could give orders again and have them carried out!

She reached the top quickly. The flat disc of the pedestal top curled up and inward all around to make it impossible for her to fall off. That left the room itself. Uncolored, it was a natural gray-red and perfectly square. She walked completely around it looking for entry, but her first assessment had been correct: it was locked up tight.

"What do you propose at this point?" Arion asked her, as he followed her around the perimeter of the room.

"We're going to have to get inside," she said, "and see what there is to see. I suppose there's no other way to get in except by using the torch?"

"Normally, this situation would never arise," Arion told her. "There are no other buildings in the city that behave like this. There is no reason to seal up a room."

"You mean you don't know why or how the rooms have sealed themselves up?"

"The city program was given to us intact through the central core, and only the central core contains the program information. Other than through observation, we don't know exactly how the city operates."

Katherine was taken aback. "So, the city is actually a highly advanced autonomous robot in its own right, operating outside of your control."

"Your statement is basically inaccurate, but containing the germ of truth," Arion said. "To begin with, it is not highly advanced, at least not in the same sense that a . . . supervisor robot, for example, is highly advanced."

"Do I detect a shade of rivalry here?" she asked.

"Certainly not," Arion said. "We are not capable of such feelings as competitiveness. I was simply stating a known fact. Furthermore, the city's autonomy is tied directly to the central core. Although it does, in fact, operate outside of supervisor control."

"Can you affect the city program, then?"

"Not directly," Arion said, running his pincers up and down the contours of the building as if checking for openings. "The central core controls the city program, and the supervisors do not make policy by direct programming."

"I think I'm beginning to truly understand," Katherine said, motioning for the robot with the torch to come closer. "The data contained in the central core is the well from which your entire city springs. All of your activities here are merely an extension of the programming contained therein, for good or ill."

"We are robots, Friend Katherine," Arion said. "It could not be otherwise. Robots are not forces of change, but merely extensions of extant thought. That is why we so desperately need the companionship of humans."

"Cut here," Katherine said pointing to the wall, and the utility robot waited until she had backed away to a safer distance before charging the power packs and moving close with the nozzle-like hose that was the business end of the laser torch. She turned to Arion. "Does cutting through the wall like this break contact with the main program?"

"No," the robot answered as the torch came on with a whine, its beam invisible as a small section of the wall glowed bright red, smoking slightly. "The synapses simply reroute themselves and make connection elsewhere."

There was a sound of suction as the torch broke through to the other side of the wall, a sound that any Spacer knew well, the rushing of air into a vacuum. The room had sealed totally and airlessly. The torch moved more quickly now, cutting a circular hole just large enough for a human being to get through without working at it.

The edges tore jaggedly, the walls that seemed so fluid under program fighting tenaciously to hold together otherwise. Despite Arion's claims, Katherine was still impressed with the city-robot.

The welder was halfway done, pulling down the jagged slab of city as he cut. Katherine had to fight down the urge to run up and peer through the opening already made, but her fear of the torch ultimately won out over her impatience.

"Are you capable of doing autopsies here?" she asked Arion as an afterthought.

"The medical programming is in existence, and at this very moment several medically trained robots are being turned out of our production facilities, along with diagnostic tables and a number of machines. Synthesized drugs and instruments are coming at a slower rate. So much of the city is geared toward building right now, and these considerations never became a problem for us until David's death."

"Done," the utility robot said, the cut section falling to clang on the base disc.

"Witness!" Arion called, as Katherine hurried to the place and climbed through the hole.

The naked body lay, face down, in the middle of the floor. Katherine walked boldly toward it, then stopped, a hand going to her chest. She had been so intent upon fulfilling her mission that she had failed to consider that it was death— real death—she'd be dealing with. It horrified her. She began shaking, her heart rate increasing.

"Is something wrong?" Eve asked from the cut-out.

"N-no," she replied, her eyes glued to the body, unable either to move forward or pull back.

"If there's a problem," she heard Arion say, "come out now. Don't jeopardize yourself."

Come on, old girl. Get yourself together. "I'm fine," she said. *You've got to do this. Don't stop now.*

She took a deep breath, then another, and continued her walk to the body. Bending, she touched it gingerly. The surface was cool, the muscles tight.

"Is everything all right?" Arion asked.

"Yes," she said. *Won't they leave me alone?*

There was no sign of decomposition, and she realized that it was because the room had been airless. At least that was something.

She examined the body from the back, her heart rate still up, her breath coming fast. Looking at the foot, she could see a small cut on the left instep and realized immediately what had caused it. Something stupid. Something she had done herself before. A misstep, perhaps a broken fall, and the bare feet came together, a too-long toenail on the other foot scraping the instep. It was nothing. There was some dried blood on the side and bottom of the foot, but that was it. She was going to have to roll the body over.

She moved to the side of the body, reaching out to try and turn it over, finding her hands shaking wildly. *Will this be me soon—fifty kilos of dead meat?* She tried to push the body onto its back, but there was no strength in her arms.

"Could you help me with this?" she called over her shoulder. Arion came through the cut-out to bend down beside her. She looked up at the nearly human-looking machine. "I want to roll it over."

"Surely," Arion said, reaching out with his pincers to push gently against the side of the body. It rolled over easily, dead eyes staring straight at Katherine.

She heard herself screaming from far away as the shock of recognition hit her. It was Derec! Derec!

The room began spinning as she felt it in her stomach and in her head. Then she felt the floor reach up and pull her down; everything else was lost in the numbing bliss of unconsciousness.

"Don't try to leave without me to lead you!" Avernus called to Derec as the boy waded into the churning sea of robots. "You could become hopelessly lost in these tunnels."

"Don't worry!" Derec called back, thinking more about the danger of the main chamber than the labyrinthine caves.

He moved slowly through the throng, walking toward Rydberg. It was damp, musty in there, plus a bit claustrophobic, but Derec was so fascinated by the spectacle of the eleventh-hour plans that he never allowed his mind to dwell on the all-too-human problems of the location.

Rydberg saw him approaching, and turned to stare as Derec closed on him. He climbed atop the cart and joined the supervisor.

"What are you doing here?" Rydberg asked, the words crackling through the speaker atop his dome. "It is too dangerous underground for you."

"I talked Avernus into bringing me down and protecting me," Derec replied. "What's going on here?"

"We're trying to tunnel up to the reservoir," Rydberg said. "We are trying to work out a way to drain off some of the reservoir into the deserted tunnels below to keep it from flooding."

Derec felt an electric charge run through him. "That's wonderful!" he yelled. "You've made a third-level connection—a creative leap!"

"It was only logical. Since the water was going to come into the mines anyway, it only made sense that we should try to direct it to parts of the mines that would cause the least amount of damage. Unfortunately, our estimates show such a move could only hold off the inevitable for a day or two longer. It may all be in vain."

"Why are you digging by hand?" Derec asked. "Where are the machines?"

"They are tied up in the mining process," Rydberg said. "The current rate of city-building must take precedence over all other activities." The robot turned his dome to watch the excavations.

Derec put his hands on the robot's arm. "But the city-building is what's killing you!"

"It must be done."

"Why?"

"I cannot answer that."

Derec looked all around him, at the frantic rush of momentum, at a civilization trying to survive. No, they weren't human, but it didn't mean their lives weren't worthwhile. What was the gauge? There was intelligence, and a concerted effort toward perfection of spirit. There was more worth, more human value here in the mines than in anything he had seen in his brief glimpse of humanity. And then it struck him, the reason for all of this and the reason for the state of emergency and security.

"It's defensive, isn't it?" he said. "The city-building is a way for the city to defend itself against alien invasion?"

Rydberg just stared at him.

He grabbed the robot's arm again, tighter. "That *is* it, isn't it?"

"I cannot answer that question."

"Then tell me I am wrong!"

"I cannot answer that question."

"I knew it," he said, convinced now. "And if it coincided with David's appearance in the city, then it is somehow tied to him. For once, Katherine's in the right place.

"This whole thing is a central core program," Derec said, "and obviously the program is in error. There must be some way you can circumvent it."

"Robots do not make programs, Derec," Rydberg said.

"Then let me into it!"

"I cannot," Rydberg replied, then added softly. "I'm sorry."

Derec just stared at him, wanting to argue him into compliance, and fearing that the argument would simply present the robot with a contradiction so vast it would freeze his mental facilities and lock him up beyond hope. He didn't know where to go from here. He'd had a tantalizing glimpse of the problem, yet, like a holographic image, it still eluded his grasp.

"You still have not told me why you came down into the mines," Rydberg said. "Humans have such a poor sense of personal danger that I fail to see how your species has survived to this point. If you cannot present me a compelling reason for your presence, I fear I must send you away now."

"If humans have a poor sense of personal danger," Derec said, angry at Robot City's inability even to try to save itself, "then it has been justly inherited in *your* programming. I've come down to visit 1-1 on a matter not of your concern. Would you please point him out to me?"

"Our first citizen?" Rydberg said, and Derec could tell the robot wanted to say more. Instead, he turned up his volume. "WILL ROBOT 1-1 PLEASE COME FORWARD."

Within a minute, a small, rather innocuous utility robot with large, powerful looking pincer grips moved up to the cart. "I am here, Supervisor Rydberg," the robot said.

"Friend Derec wishes to speak with you on a personal matter," the supervisor said. "Do as he asks, but do not take an excessive amount of time."

Derec jumped off the cart. "I hear you were the first robot awakened on this planet," he said.

"That is correct," the robot said.

"Come with me," Derec said. "Let's get out of the confusion."

They moved through the rapidly widening chamber to the place where Avernus had first dropped him. "I am searching through the origins of Robot City," Derec said, "and that search has led me to you. You were the first."

"Yes. Logical. I was the first."

"I want you to tell me exactly what your first visual input was and what followed subsequently."

"My first visual input was of a human arm connecting my power supply," the robot said. "Then the human turned and walked away from me."

"Did you see the human face?"

"No."

"What happened then?"

"The human walked a distance from me, then disappeared behind some machinery meant to help in our early mining. I was to wait for one hour, then turn on the other inoperative robots in the area. Then we were to begin work, which we did."

"Of what did that original work consist?"

"There were fifty utility, plus Supervisor Avernus. Twenty-five of us built the Compass Tower from materials left for us, while Supervisor Avernus and the other twenty-five began the design and construction of the underground facilities and commenced the mining operations."

Derec was puzzled. "Avernus didn't supervise the construction of the Compass Tower?"

"No. It was meant as a separate entity from the rest of the city. It was fully planned, fully materialized. There was no need for Supervisor Avernus to take an interest in it."

Derec heard an engine noise and saw lights, far in the tunnel distance, gradually closing on his position. "What do you mean when you say it was 'meant as a separate entity'?" Derec asked.

"The Compass Tower is unique in several respects, Friend Derec," 1-1 said. "It is not part of the overall city plan in any respect; it has the off limits homing platform atop it; and it contains a fully furnished, human administration office."

"What!" Derec said loudly, as he watched the mine tram rushing closer toward him in the tunnel. "An office for whom?"

"I do not know. Perhaps the person who awakened me."

"You've never spoken of this with the supervisors?"

"No one has ever inquired before now."

"Why did you call it the administration office?"

"The construction plans are locked within my data banks," 1-1 answered. "That is what it was called on the plans."

The tram car screeched to a halt right beside Darren, the huge bulk of Avernus stuffed in its front seat. "We must go," the supervisor said.

"Just a minute," Derec said. "Why did you call it a homing platform?"

"We must go now," Avernus said.

"It was designed as a landing point of some kind," l-1 said. "Nothing is ever allowed on its surface, or within twenty meters of its airspace."

Avernus took hold of Derec's arm and gently, but firmly, turned him face to face. "We must go," Avernus said. "Something has happened to Friend Katherine."

Derec reeled as if he'd been hit. "What? What happened? Is she all right?"

"She is unconscious," Avernus said. "Beyond that, we do not know."

Derec hurried into the apartment to buzzing activity. Arion was there, and Euler, plus Eve and several utility robots. There was also a rather frail-looking machine with multiple appendages that Derec surmised to be a med-bot.

The living room seemed different, much squatter, but he really wasn't paying attention.

"Friend Derec . . ." Euler began, hurrying to intercept Derec as he crossed the living room floor.

"Where is she?" he asked, still moving.

"The bedroom," Euler said. "She has regained consciousness and is resting. I do not think you should try and see her just yet."

"Nonsense," Derec said, hurrying past him. "I've *got* to see her."

"But you don't underst . . ."

"Later," Derec said, moving down the hallway. There were now two bedroom doors. He opened one to an empty room, then turned to the other, pushing the stud. It slid open. Katherine was sitting up in bed, her face drained of all color, her eyes red.

"Are you all right?" he asked.

Her eyes focused on him, then grew wide in horror.

"Noooo!" she screamed, hands going to her straining face.

Derec ran to her and took her by the shoulders. She kept screaming, loudly, hysterically, her body vibrating madly on the bed.

"You're dead!" she yelled. "Dead! Dead!"

"No!" he yelled. "I'm here. It's all right. It's all . . ."

Euler was pulling him away from her, robots filling the room. "What are you doing?" he yelled. "Let go, I . . ."

"You must leave now," Euler said, lifting him bodily in the air and carrying him, Katherine's screams still filling the apartment.

"Katherine!" he called to her as Euler carried him out the door. "Katherine!"

Euler carried him all the way to the living room, then simply held him there, the med-bot slipping into her bedroom and sliding the door closed, muffling the screams somewhat.

"Put me down!" Derec yelled. "Would you put me down?"

"You must not go in there," Euler said. "It is dangerous for Katherine if you go in there."

He felt the anger draining out of him. "What's going on?" he asked sheepishly. "What's happened to her?"

"She's suffered some sort of emotional trauma," the supervisor said. "May I put you down?"

"Believe me," Derec said, "at this point, I don't want to go back in."

Euler set him gently on the floor. Derec rubbed his arms to get the circulation back into them.

"I am sorry if I caused you any discomfort," Euler said. "Truly."

"It's all right," Derec replied. "Tell me what happened."

Thunder crashed loudly outside, both Derec and Euler turning to look at the building thunderheads through the open patio door. They were in for another bad one. From the bedroom, the sounds of screaming had died to occasional whimpers.

"Katherine found the body of David," Euler said, "and had a utility robot cut into the sealed room that contained it." The robot swiveled its head to take in the rest of the room. "Perhaps it is better to have Arion witness the story. He was present for it." He motioned for the human-like machine to join the discussion.

"Friend Derec," Arion said as he moved up close. "I had no idea that seeing the body would have this kind of effect on Friend Katherine. I would never have allowed her to come close to it had I known."

"I understand," Derec said. "Just tell me what happened."

"She was examining the deceased," Arion said, "when she called me in to help her roll the body over. I, of course, complied. She screamed when she saw the face, then lapsed into a state of unconsciousness."

"She's been disconsolate ever since," Euler said. "Most peculiar. She persisted in the belief that the dead man was you."

"Why would she do that?" he asked, moving to sit at the table. Arion's CRT was busily finding the cube roots of ten-digit numbers.

"I don't know," Euler said. "Perhaps because the body looked like yours."

Derec sat up straight, staring hard. "You mean . . . just like me?"

The robots looked at one another. "Perfectly," Arion said.

"Doesn't that strike you as odd?" Derec said, dumb-founded, still not believing the information.

"No," Euler said.

"I don't understand," Derec said. "When you first saw me, didn't you take note of the similarity of our appearances?"

"Yes," Euler said, "but it didn't mean anything to us."

"Why not?"

Arion spoke up. "Why should it? We've only seen three human beings. Robots certainly can look exactly alike, why not humans? We knew you and Katherine were different, but that didn't mean that you and David couldn't be the same. Besides, we *knew* that David was dead; so, consequently, we *knew* that you couldn't be David. Simple."

The med-bot came gliding down the hall, moving quickly

up to Derec. "She's calm now," the robot said. "She's lightly sedated with her own pituitary endorphins, and wants to see you."

Derec stood, uneasy after the last time. "It'll be all right?" he asked the med-bot.

"I believe she understands the situation now," the med-bot responded in a gentle, fatherly voice.

"I'd like to see her alone," he told the others.

Euler nodded. "We'll wait out here."

He moved down the hall, unsure of his feelings. It had hurt him to see her in such pain, hurt him emotionally. She could get on his nerves so badly, yet seemed such an integral part of him.

He knocked lightly on her door, then opened it. She sat up in bed, her face still sad. She held her arms out to him. "Oh, Derec . . ."

He hurried to the bed, sitting next to her, holding her. She began to sob gently into his shoulder. "I was so afraid," she said. "I thought . . . thought . . ."

"I know," he said, stroking her hair. "Arion told me. I'm so sorry."

"I don't know what I'd do without you," she said, then pulled away from him. "Oh, Derec. I know we've walls between us . . . but please believe me, I have no idea what this place is and what's going on here."

"I believe you," he said, reaching up to wipe tears from her eyes. He smiled. "Don't worry about that now. How are you doing?"

"Better," she said. "The med-bot stuck me a couple of times, but it really helped. All I've got is a headache."

Thunder rolled again outside. "Good," he said. "It looks like we're locked in for the night anyway. What do you say we send the robots away, get some dinner sent up, and compare notes. I've got a lot to tell you."

"Me, too," she said. "It sounds good."

* * *

They had a vegetable soup for dinner that was the best thing Derec had eaten for quite some time. The rains pounded frenetically outside, but Derec didn't worry so much since he figured the precautions taken by Euler and Rydberg would, at least, get them through the night. And the best he could do now was to live day to day. Even Arion's entertainment was beginning to diversify. The CRT was exhibiting an animated game of tennis played by computer-generated stick figures on a slippery surface. It was actually quite amusing.

After the servo had cleared the dishes away and left, they made themselves comfortable on the couch and recounted the details of the day. Derec, for reasons he wasn't quite sure of, left out the fact that there were no hyperwave transmission stations on the planet. Counting on Katherine's experiences to help him, he listened alertly to her account of the discovery of the body.

"The fact that he looked just like you," she asked when she'd finished, "what does it mean?"

"To begin with," he said, "it finally knocks the idea of our trip to Robot City being an accident right out the air lock. We were brought here; why, I don't know. The dead man is either the one who brought us or was brought himself. We'll have to continue to ferret that out. What interests me more is the fact that the city-robot works independently. I believe that the city is somehow replicating itself as a defensive measure. If it operates independently, the supervisors may not be *able* to stop it."

"What does that mean?"

He looked at her. "It means that I've got to."

"That brings us back to our same old argument," she said, darkening a bit. "The city or the murder investigation."

"Not necessarily," he said, standing. "This should make you happy." He walked back to the patio door and idly watched the downpour, feeling now that it could, eventually, be beaten. He turned back to her. "I believe that David and the city alert and replication are inexorably linked."

She jumped up, excited, and ran to him, throwing her arms around him. "You're going to help me solve the murder, aren't you?"

"Yes," he laughed, returning the embrace. "Tomorrow we go back to the body and pick up where you left off." He moved away from her and intertwined his fingers. "It's all like this, all connected. If we can put a few of the pieces together, I'll bet the rest fall into place. Whatever, or whoever, killed David, is the reason for the alert."

"First thing in the morning, we'll have Eve take us back there."

"Not first thing," he said. "First thing, I've set up a brief meeting with the supervisors at the Compass Tower."

"Why?"

"Two reasons. First, I want to ask them some questions about their underground operations; and second, I want to be able to poke around the building for a bit."

"Looking for the office?"

He nodded. "1-l said it was fully furnished. I bet we'll find answers there."

Her face got suddenly serious. "I hope you find the kind of answers you're looking for," she said.

A table had been set up in the meeting room. It was long and narrow and included seats for nine. Derec sat at the head of the table, with Katherine at his right. The supervisors took up the rest of the seats, still holding hands, with the two at the end of the line holding hands over the tabletop.

"Why do human beings lie, Friend Derec?" Supervisor Dante asked, his elongated, magnifying eyes staring all the way down the table. "The most difficulty we've had with you is your penchant for lies and exaggeration. It is what keeps us from trusting you completely."

Derec licked dry lips and watched them all expectantly watching him. He knew he'd have to get beyond this hurdle if he were to work with them in solving the city's problems.

"Robots receive their input in two ways," he said, hoping his explanation would be adequate. He'd gotten up early to think it out and prepare it. "Through direct programming, and through input garnered through the sensors that is then tested in analog against existing programming. Your sensors record events accurately, with mathematic precision, and classify them through the scientific validity of several thousand years of empirical thought. You are then able, through your positronics, to reason deductively by weighing, again through analog, incoming data against existing data. You can make true second-level connections."

"We understand the workings of the positronic brain," Friend Derec," Waldeyer said. "It is the human brain that confounds us."

"Bear with me," Derec said. "I want to pose you a question. Suppose, just suppose, that your basic programming was in error—not just in small ways, but in its most basic assumptions. Suppose every bit of sensory input you received was in total opposition to your basic programming."

"We would spend a great deal of time reasoning erroneously," Wohler said. "But human brains are not at the mercy of programming. You have the freedom to sift through all empirical data and arrive at the truth at all times."

"That's where you are wrong," Derec replied. "The human mind is not a computer with truth as its base. It is merely a collection of ganglia moved by electrical impulses. Truth is not its basis, but rather ego gratification. Truth to the human mind is a shifting thing, a sail billowing on the wind of fear and hope and desire. It has no reality, but rather creates it from moment to moment with that same creative intelligence that you value so highly in us."

"But the base program is available," Euler said. "It is there for the human to use."

"And it is also there for him to reject," Derec countered. "You *must* observe your programming. My mind has no such chains on it. The human mind is painfully mortal. That particular truth in itself is more than most humans can tolerate. We are frail creatures, seeking permanence in an impermanent world. We lie to those around us. We lie to ourselves. We lie in the face of all logic and all reason. We lie because, quite often, the truth would destroy us. We lie without even knowing it."

Avernus spoke. "How do robots that exist with humans on other worlds deal with the deceit?"

"They follow instruction according to the Laws of Robotics," Derec said, quite simply. "They are not autonomous as you are, so they have no choice. The Laws were invented with the salvation of the species in mind. Robots protect humans from their own lies, and honor them because of what's noble in the species. You saw Katherine's grief when she thought I was dead." He reached out and took her hand. "We are fragile creatures capable of great nobility and great ignominy. We make no excuses for ourselves. We are the creators of great good and great evil, and in the creation of robots, we were at the height of our goodness. Our species deserves praise and condemnation, and, in the final analysis, it is beyond rational, positronic explanation."

"You are saying we must take you as you are," Euler said.

"No laws will define us," Derec answered, "no theorem hold us in check. We will amaze and confound you, but I can guarantee you we will never be boring."

"You would tame us with your words," Wohler, the philosopher, said.

"Yes," Derec said, smiling. "I would do exactly that. And I will tell you now that you will let me because the wonders of the universe are contained in my confounding mind, and you can only reach them through me . . . and you desperately want to reach them!"

"But what of the Laws of Humanics?" Rydberg asked.

"Very simple," Katherine added, winking at Derec. "There is only one Law of Humanics: expect the unexpected."

"An oxymoron," Arion said.

"As close as you'll ever get," Derec said. "That's the point. You needn't give up your search for the Laws of Humanics, but you must make them fit us, not try to make us fit them. We can't be anything but what we are, but if you accept us—good and bad—we'll see to it that you reach your full potential."

"Intriguing words," Dante said, "but just words. Where is an example of what you can do with your creative intelligence?"

"If you'll let me," Derec said, "perhaps I can help you save your city."

"All your suggestions so far have tried to force us away

from our programming," Euler said.

Derec stood; he thought better on his feet. "That's because until yesterday I never fully realized what was going on and how little control you had over the situation. I'm working on that, too, but I have some other ideas."

Arion and Waldeyer sat side by side, pincers locked together. Derec walked between the two of them, resting his elbows on their shoulders.

"I've watched you digging in the tunnels, trying to siphon off reservoir water to lower the level and avoid a flooding of your underground operations. Has it been successful?"

"To a degree," Rydberg said. "We will break through after our meeting this morning. Unfortunately, we calculate that it will only postpone the inevitable for one more day. We can save our operations through tonight's expected rain, but that's it."

"All right," Derec said. "Let's think about something. I was in the main chamber of one of the quadrants yesterday. Was that chamber dug?"

"No," Avernus said. "Each quadrant Extruder Station is located in a chamber similiar to that one. Our first action in beginning underground operations was to take sonogram readings to determine natural caverns under the surface. The mine tunnels were dug, but the main chambers are natural."

"Has it occurred to you," Derec said, "to take sonograms now, in the present situation?"

"I do not understand," Avernus said.

Derec pounded the tabletop with an index finger. "Find the closest underground cavern to your reservoir, dig a tunnel connecting it to the reservoir, and . . ."

"And drain the reservoir water in there!" Avernus said, standing abruptly and breaking contact with the central core.

"Right!" Derec pointed to him. "Meanwhile, Katherine and I will be working on solving the murder. I'm absolutely convinced that the solution to the murder will also provide the reasons for the state of emergency." He turned to Supervisor Dante. "Is *that* creative enough for you?"

"Happily so," Dante said.

"It seems," Euler said, "that if we are to have the opportunity of putting Friend Derec's suggestions into practice, we should adjourn this meeting and set to work."

The robots stood, Derec wondering if they realized that he had gently manipulated them, for the first time, into including him as a real partner in their planning.

He watched them filing out of the large room, for the first time beginning to feel he was getting a handle on the deviousness of the mind that had brought all of them together. Synnoetics. The worst hills still remained to be scaled toward reaching a truly equal social union of human and robot. Now, if they could only survive the rains, they could perhaps be the trailblazers in the opening of a new era.

As soon as the robots left the room, Katherine hurried to the door and peered out. "They're gone," she said, turning back to Derec.

"Good."

He joined her at the door, Eve and Rec, trailing dutifully. Derec turned to them. "Has either of you ever witnessed within this building before?"

"Yes," Rec said. "Most of this building is given to experimentation on the positronic brain and ways to improve its function. I have witnessed experiments in almost every laboratory in the structure."

"Have you ever seen an office, something that a human might use as his personal quarters?"

"No," the robot answered.

"Are there parts of the building you have never seen?"

"Yes."

"All right, listen carefully," Derec said, shrugging in Katherine's direction. "I want you to take me to all the parts of the building you have never seen."

"I cannot do that."

"Why not?" Katherine asked.

"There is a sector in the Compass Tower that is off-limits to robots. No one goes there."

"Did someone tell you that," Derec asked, "a supervisor?"

"It is part of our programming," Rec said.

Eve agreed. "Not even supervisors are allowed."

Derec shook his head. Just like robots—all duty, no inquisitiveness. "I want you to take us there," he said.

"I already told you it was off-limits," Rec said.

Derec smiled. "I don't mean for you to take me *inside* the off-limits part," he said. "Just take me as close as you can get and point it out to me."

That seemed amenable enough, so the two witnesses led the way, while Derec and Katherine followed closely. They walked the maze-like halls, twisting and turning, but always going higher. An elevator took them six floors up, but that wasn't even the end of it. It was interesting to Derec. The meeting room had been designed to look like it was at the apex of the pyramid, but it was actually only about halfway up the structure, perhaps the illusion being more spiritual in intent than anything else.

The upper levels had begun to get rather small, doorways appearing more sparsely between the gently glowing wall panels, when the robots abruptly stopped. Rec pointed to a door at the end of a short hallway.

"We can go no farther," the robot said. "No one knows where that doorway leads."

"If you want to wait here," Derec said, "we'll be back soon."

"But it is off-limits," Eve said.

"To robots, not humans," Katherine replied.

"But we cannot separate," Rec persisted.

"It is only one door," Derec said. "We'll have to come back through it."

"Our orders . . ."

"Do what you want," Derec said. "We're going on."

With that, Derec and Katherine continued down the hallway, turning once to see the attentive robots before opening the door and stepping inside.

What they found was a spiral staircase leading up to a door set ten feet above their heads.

"You want to go first?" Derec asked.

"Go ahead," Katherine returned. "I left my courage back in that sealed room."

Derec moved slowly up the stairs, a feeling of expectation rising slowly in his stomach. He connected the word, butterflies, to the feeling, but had no idea of what it meant. He reached the door, and pushed the stud, expecting it to be locked up tight.

It wasn't.

The door slid easily and opened, he thought at first, to the outside. It was as if he were walking onto an open platform set with furniture and a desk, a beautiful, panoramic view of Robot City all around. But there was no feel of the air, no wind, no heat from the mid-morning sun.

"How did we get outside?" Katherine asked, following him in.

"We're not," Derec said, pointing behind her.

The outside view was marred by the still-open doorway, a black maw in the center of downtown. When he pushed the stud to close the door, the full view was restored.

"Viewscreens?" she asked.

"I think so," he replied. "There must be a series of small cameras set around the peak of the pyramid to give the view, which is then put on the screens. Look," he pointed, "even above us."

She looked up to see pinkish-blue sky above. "That would be the view from the platform we materialized on," she said.

"Fascinating," he said softly, knowing they'd finally stumbled upon something. "If you were sitting in here, you could watch someone materialize on the platform and they'd never know it."

"Do you think someone watched *us* materialize?" she asked, eyes wide.

He shrugged. "I'd have to think it probable at this point,"

he said. "We were brought here. We were *meant* to be here. It seems logical that our progress would be measured."

"Have you ever considered the fact, Derec, that *you* were brought here and I'm excess baggage?" she asked.

He walked slowly through the room. It was designed for someone to live in. There were easy chairs and a couch that converted to a bed. Not city-robot material, but real furniture. There was even a plant of some kind under its own growth light. That told Derec that whoever kept this office returned at least often enough to keep the plant watered.

"I've considered a great many things," Derec told her, "including the scenario you've just outlined. But there are several things to consider. I believe our meeting on Aranimas's ship was accidental. The situation was too dangerous and uncontrollable to be otherwise, our injuries too real. But consider the facts that you admit to having known me previously by another name and that that name just happens to belong to someone who looked enough like me to be my twin. It's a large universe, Katherine. That's an awful lot of coincidence. Let me ask you something. Have *you* ever considered the possibility that the David you knew could be the one lying dead in that sealed room, and that I'm somebody else?"

Her face became confused, lips sputtering. "I—I . . ."

Then she started to say something and stopped. Derec would have given a fortune, ten fortunes, to know the thoughts that had been running through her mind that second before she shut herself up.

"What are you hiding from me?" he asked loudly, in frustration.

Her face was a mixture of pain and longing. She responded by solidifying, as she had done so many times since they'd met on Aranimas's ship. "There's nothing up here for me," she said. "I'm going back down with the robots. Join us quickly. We have other work to do."

Then she turned and departed without a backward glance,

leaving Derec angry again. He could feel so close to her, and so far away. There was never any mid-point with Katherine; it was all one way or the other.

He decided to inspect the office methodically, rather than simply tearing furiously into things, which had been his strongest desire. Starting on the outer edges of the room, he traversed it slowly, saving the plum of the desk for last.

He found a small, air-tight shelf full of tapes, all marked "Philosophy," then broken down according to planet. Nearly all of the fifty-five Spacer worlds were represented. They weren't of interest to him at the moment, but a perusal in future wasn't out of the question.

He continued his walk of the outer perimeter, his hand finding the ladder where his eyes couldn't. It was a metal ladder, set against the screen and lost in shadows. Even knowing it was there, he still found it difficult to see. It went up from the floor and stopped at the flat ceiling.

He climbed it until he reached the ceiling screen. There was no reason at all for this ladder to exist unless it went somewhere. Gingerly, he reached out and touched the ceiling screen above the ladder. It gave easily on well-oiled hinges, flapping open to reveal real sky.

He moved up through the trap door to find himself standing on the platform where he had materialized. Amazing. He began to put together a theory. Whoever started this civilization, whoever's arm it was that turned on l-l, with proper use of a Key to Perihelion, could materialize on Robot City at will, move down into the off-limits office and observe his city's progress without ever being seen. When he was through, he could leave by the same means.

So, the city had an overseer, a guardian, who had apparently brought Derec here to sweeten the mix with the human ingredient. Why Derec? That question, he couldn't answer.

He wondered if the overseer had been present during his and Katherine's stay, if he had been watching them, perhaps all the way up to the moment they opened the office door. It would be simple enough for him to get away. All he'd need was the Key and a few seconds' time.

Derec climbed back into the office and closed the trap door behind him, once again sealing in the illusion completely.

He continued his tour of the office by emptying the small trash can that sat by the desk. The trash can held several empty containers that he recognized as standard Spacer survival rations of good-tasting roughage plus supplementary vitamin and protein pills. He torn open one of the roughage containers to find, in the corner, a small glob of the stuff, which hadn't hardened completely. This food had been eaten within the last twenty-four hours. The rest of the trash was comprised of wadded-up pieces of paper containing mathematical equations relating to the geometric progression of the city-building, which seemed to relate to the time it would take to fill the entire planet with city. Others seemed to be directed to the amounts of rainfall and the reservoir size, quick calculations regarding how long it would take an overflow to occur. Derec had the feeling that if he simply sat in the office and waited an indefinite amount of time, he could probably catch the overseer coming back. Unfortunately, he didn't have an indefinite amount of time.

He put the trash back in the can and directed his attention to the desk itself. The top of the iron-alloy desk contained a blotter with paper and two zero-g ink pens. The only personal item on the desk was a holo-cube containing a scene of a very nice looking woman holding a baby. The sight of the cube sent a cold chill down his back.

He turned his attention to the drawers. On his left were several small drawers, which were, for the most part, empty. Only the top drawer contained anything at all, and that was simply more paper and some technical data on the workings of the logic circuits of the positronic brain. On his right, however, he struck gold. As he opened the big well drawer there, a slight motor hum brought a computer terminal up to desktop level, the screen already active, the cursor flashing: READY.

Interestingly enough, the terminal had all the hook-ups and leads for hyperwave transmission and reception. Unfortunately, the power pack and directional hyperwave antenna were missing from the back, taken, no doubt, by the overseer.

He stared at the terminal in disbelief. No blocks, no passwords, no protections on the system at all. He couldn't believe that an entire civilization would open itself up to him just because he'd found an office. Suppose he'd meant to cause it harm?

Cautiously, he slipped into the scheme of things, working his way down to the level of files, then asking to go to the central core. Once reaching that, he asked to open the file marked: CITY DEFENSES.

Within seconds, the READY signal was flashing again. He was in! Rapidly he typed:

LIST CITY DEFENSES.

The computer answered:

CITY DEFENSES: ADVANCE REPLICATION
                      SEAL CONTAMINATION
                      HALT CENTRAL CORE INPUT
                      MOBILATE CENTRAL CORE
                      LOCALIZE EMERGENCY
                            TERMINALS
                      ISOLATE SUPERVISORY
                            PERSONNEL

He sat, shaking, at the typer. This was it. He decided to try his hand at shutting it down. He typed:

CANCEL REPLICATION.

The computer never hesitated.

CITY DEFENSES CANNOT BE CANCELED WITHOUT JUSTIFICATION AND INPUT REGARDING ALIEN THREAT OR CONTAMINATION.

Derec typed:

OVERRIDE ALL PREVIOUS INSTRUCTIONS AND CANCEL REPLICATION.

The computer answered:

OVERRRIDE IMPOSSIBLE UNDER ALL CIRCUM-STANCES. CITY DEFENSES CANNOT BE CANCELED WITHOUT JUSTIFICATION AND INPUT REGARDING ALIEN THREAT OR CONTAMINATION.

It was a lock-out. The computer refused even to talk to him about it unless he could determine the reason for the defensive measures and provide proper rationalization for termination. It seemed etched in granite. He typed:

LIST REASONS FOR CITY DEFENSE ACTIVATION.

The computer answered with a graph of the city, its shape ever changing, turning slowly. A tiny light was flashing in the section marked Quadrant #4. At the bottom of the screen the computer wrote:

ALIEN CONTAMINATION IN QUADRANT #4.

Derec asked:

CITE NATURE OF CONTAMINATION.

The computer answered:

ALIEN CONTAMINATION IN QUADRANT #4.

He sat back and looked at the machine. It was very possible that the flashing light could represent the body of his look-alike. The machine wasn't going to let him off the hook on the murder. He was beginning to see why it was so easy for him to get into the central core from this terminal, and he received his final confirmation quickly, when he typed:

LIST PROCEDURE FOR DEACTIVATION OF CITY DEFENSES.

The machine replied:

DEACTIVATION PROCEDURE:

>   ISOLATE CONTAMINATION OR
>   PRESENCE
>   DEFINE NATURE OF THREAT
>   NEUTRALIZE THREAT
>   PROVIDE PROOF OF

NEUTRALIZATION THRU
PROCEDURE C-15

Derec typed:
LIST PROCEDURE C-15
And was answered:
PROCEDURE C-15:   ISOLATE MOBILATED
CENTRAL CORE
ENTER CENTRAL CORE
PROVIDE SUPERVISOR
PASSWORD
ENTER PROOF OF
NEUTRALIZATION

Derec just stared at the screen, frustrated and amazed at
what he was looking at. Nothing of consequence could be
done from this terminal, or from *any* city terminal, for that
matter. Input had to come directly at the central core, and
unless he misunderstood the word "mobilate," the central
core was not stationary. It was mobile, moving. And to
round out the entire business philosophically, a supervisor
robot was necessary to enter the defensive program.

It was actually the perfect defense. The act of shutting
down the defenses had to be deliberate and calculated and
agreed to by *both* human and robot supervision. Again,
the system was set up synnoetically, and Derec, despite his
disappointment, had to admire it. Ultimately, he really
didn't know the form of the contamination. The central
core was behaving properly by not granting his requests
for deactivation until all the facts were in. The problem,
of course, was that city could kill itself before the facts
came to light.

He was back where he started, with the murder of his
twin. There was still much he could learn from the office
and the open terminal, but he simply didn't have the time
right now. He reluctantly decided that he'd have to close out
for now and return when there was more time.

He had reached out to return the terminal to its berth in

the drawer when he thought of something. If the overseer were, indeed, keeping track of them, perhaps there was a file extant with that information. Not knowing his own name, he decided to go with another. Bringing the filename menu back on the screen, he typed in the words:

BURGESS, KATHERINE

The machine answered:

BURGESS, KATHERINE, see DAVID.

His mouth was dry, his heart pounding as he typed in the name of the dead man.

The machine answered quickly, in a notation file obviously set in the overseer's own hand:

ASSIMILATION TEST ON DAVID #2 PROCEEDED ON LINE AND WITHOUT MISHAP UNTIL THE TRIGGERING OF THE CITY DEFENSIVE SYSTEM AND THE DEATH OF SUBJECT THROUGH UNKNOWN MEANS.

WITHOUT HUMAN INTERVENTION, ROBOTS ARE UNABLE TO PREVENT VITAL DAMAGE THROUGH OVER-SUCCESS OF CITY PLANNING AND OPERATION WOULD BE TOTAL FAILURE.

DAVID #1 ARRIVED TO INTERVENE IN CITY CATASTROPHE AND PROCEED WITH ORIGINAL OPERATIONAL TESTING OF SYNNOETIC THEORIES. RESULTS YET TO BE SEEN.

UNCONTROLLED FACTOR ARRIVED WITH DAVID #1 IN THE FORM OF A WOMAN. SHE IS NOW CALLING HERSELF KATHERINE BURGESS FOR REASONS UNKNOWN. HER ULTIMATE INFLUENCE OVER OPERATION AND THE EXACT NATURE OF HER AIMS HAVE YET TO BE DETERMINED.

SHE WILL BE WATCHED CAREFULLY.

That was it, the end of the file. Derec stared at the flashing cursor for a moment, his mind whirling with a dozen different thoughts. But one thought overrode everything else, one sentence burned its way into his brain and hurt him

more deeply than he thought possible—SHE IS NOW
CALLING HERSELF KATHERINE BURGESS FOR REA-
SONS UNKNOWN.

CHAPTER 10
THE SEALED ROOM

Derec had hoped that when he came out of the overseer's office Katherine would have already been gone, but she wasn't. She stood waiting for him with the two witness robots, a smile on her face as if seeing him somehow made her happy. What an actress. He had to wonder now, once again, what it was she wanted out of all this. He'd once again have to pull in and play it by ear where she was concerned. Perhaps she'd say something to give herself away. Meanwhile, she'd get no satisfaction.

"How did it go?" she asked cheerily, but then her face changed, tightened up when she noticed his mood swing. "What's wrong?"

"Nothing . . . Katherine," he said, her phony name sticking in his throat. "I found an exit to the top platform, and a computer, but nothing in it helped any, except to tell me what we already knew—that we'd have to solve the murder."

"Well then, I think we should stop wasting time and get on to that," she said suspiciously, not quite believing his change of attitude. "Are you sure you're okay?"

"Never better," he lied, angry at himself for wanting to be close to her despite what he'd learned. If he had any sense, he'd turn and run as fast and as far as he could from her. Instead, he said, "Let's go."

They moved out of the Compass Tower quickly and quietly, Katherine watching Derec out of the corner of her eye most of the time. He tried to be more nonchalant to keep from arousing her suspicions, but it was difficult for him. He apparently wasn't as schooled in subterfuge as she. As they made their way through the building, robots paid them no attention, already becoming familiar and comfortable with human presence.

When they stepped outside, they found a tram with a utility driver atop it, waving to them. "Friend Derec!" the robot called, and they moved over to the tram.

"What is it?" Derec asked the squat driver.

"Supervisor Euler asked me to be your driver today, honoring an earlier request you made in regard to transportation."

"Well," Derec said, looking at Katherine, "it appears that we're finally being trusted a little bit. Our own tram, eh?"

"It's radio-controlled," the utility robot said.

Derec narrowed his brows. "What's its range?"

"The range of the control is roughly equivalent to the limits of the already extruded city."

"Oh," Derec said quietly. "You mean that the tram won't operate except in city limits?"

"A fair appraisal," the robot said.

Katherine laughed loudly. "Now *that's* what I call trust," she said, and shook her head.

He glared at her and climbed into the tram. "Rec," he told his witness, "why don't you ride up here with me?"

The robot dutifully climbed in beside Derec, leaving Katherine to sit with her witness in the seat behind.

"Where to, sir?" the tram driver asked.

Derec turned to Katherine. "You know where we're going?"

"Quadrant #4," Katherine replied. "Eve will show you from there."

They drove on quickly. Derec, for the first time, took a moment to think about the other things that had happened in the office, things that were pushed out of his mind by his anger toward Katherine. His name, for instance. He was called David #1 on the computer record. Then why did he come *after* David #2? Was it a simple experiment shorthand, or did the name have meaning? It sounded so . . . engineered. The thoughts generated by that line of reasoning were more than he could bear. He pushed them away and thought that if his name was, indeed, David, then Katherine *had* told him the truth; at least about that.

There were other concepts implied in those few paragraphs. Whoever the overseer was, he obviously knew David and Katherine, and knew something of their past histories. So whoever had brought him here was someone he'd known before his memory loss, and he couldn't help but consider the possibility that the overseer had had something to do with his memory loss. But the chances were just as good, if not better, that Katherine herself had been connected with his amnesia for her own purposes, whatever they were.

Layers and layers. So much had been implied by the notes on the computer. The city was, indeed, considered an experiment in synnoetics, of that much he could now be certain. But then, when it came time to deal with a reason for the defense system going operational, the overseer seemed just as much in the dark as he, himself, was.

Derec also wasn't sure if he had been deliberately brought here to help the city, or if he had shown up accidentally, the overseer deciding to use him, as opposed to either stepping in himself or letting the operation shut itself down. The more answers he found, it seemed, the more in the dark he was.

They arrived at quadrant #4 without difficulty. Eve took her triangulation readings to help them find their way back to the house on the pedestal. Derec watched the city developing all around him as they drove, the sight of humans driving the inhabitants into a frenzy of human preparation—the robot equivalent of nesting.

"This is the place," Eve said as the tram stopped in the middle of an ordinary-looking street. The witness looked all around. "It doesn't appear to be here."

"It's moved some, that's all," Katherine said. "We'll go on foot from this point."

They climbed out of the tram and started walking, the tram following close behind them in case they had need of it.

"You sure this is the right direction?" Derec asked, after they had gone a block. "How far could it have moved?"

"Everything looks familiar here," she replied.

"The whole city looks the same," Derec said. "I don't think you . . ."

"There!" She pointed.

Derec needed no pointing finger to tell him they'd arrived. A tall tower stood in the middle of a street, nothing else anywhere near it. Atop the tower was a single room, sealed up except for a circular hole cut out of it.

"Let's leave a witness here with the tram in case of problems," Derec said. "We'll take Rec up with us."

"Fine," Katherine replied, walking to the pole.

He followed her, watching the spiral staircase reform when she touched the pole with her hand.

"You're not going to believe this," she told him, starting confidently up the stairs. "If this man's not your twin, he went to an awful lot of trouble to look just like you."

Derec smiled weakly in return, wondering, given the fact that he was #1, just who was whose twin.

She reached the top, waiting off to the side for him to join her. "I want you to go in first," she said. "After what happened last time, I'm afraid of my reactions. I may have to work up to it."

"All right," he said, moving around to the cut-out. As he got close to the place, he felt his own insides jumping a bit at the thought of seeing himself dead. He got right up to the cut-out, then quickly ducked his head in before he changed his mind.

It was empty.

He climbed through; there was no sign of a body or anything that resembled a body or anything else for that matter.

"Katherine," he called. "Come around here."

She moved to the cut-out, shyly poking her head inside, her eyes widening when she saw the empty room. "Where is he?" she asked.

"That was my question," Derec replied. "It appears that our corpse has gotten up and walked away.

"Or was taken away," she returned. "Remember what happened when he died? A utility robot had to fight waste control robots for possession of the corpse. Maybe they got him this time."

"Didn't anyone stay behind when you passed out before to keep that from happening?"

"I don't know," Katherine said, and went back out the cut-out to call down to her witness. "Eve! Did anyone stay behind after I fell unconscious yesterday?"

"No," the robot called back up. "You were our first priority. We all did our parts to get you home safely and to get you medical attention."

Katherine came back into the room. "No one stayed behind," she said.

"I heard," Derec replied. "Pretty convenient."

"Convenient for whom?" she said, eyes flashing. "What are you driving at?"

"Nothing," he replied. "I'm just . . . disappointed."

"*You're* disappointed," she said, sitting on the floor and leaning against the wall. "This was my ticket out of here."

"Just like you," he said, "thinking about yourself while the whole world crumbles around you."

Her eyes were dark fire. "And just who should I think about?" she asked. "The buckets of bolts who run this place, who don't have enough sense to keep from destroying themselves?"

"Like every other human culture that ever lived," he replied. "Yes. Think about them . . ." He pointed at her, then snapped his fingers. "Maybe we don't need a body for this.

Maybe we can simply recreate the circumstances."

"You mean try and set it all up just like it happened to the dead man?"

"Sure. The computer in the office told me that there is danger from alien contamination. Let's see if we can bring it out a little."

Katherine stood again, her face uncertain. "Need I remind you that the last man who had to face up to this predicament is dead?"

He walked past her, out onto the now inward-curled disc that held the room, watching the robots on the streets hurrying to their deadlines through time and space. She joined him within a minute.

"What choice do we have?" he asked.

"None," she answered. "Both of our problems are tied up in the murder. We'll do whatever we have to, to solve it."

"Let's go over everything the witness told you," Derec said. "Look for a loophole."

"It's sparse," Katherine replied. "He was already sealed up, and angry about it, when they arrived to cut him out. He had no idea why he'd been sealed in. When they cut him out, his behavior seemed a bit erratic, he had a headache and a cut on his foot."

"Didn't you have a headache last night?" he asked.

She cocked her head. "I just assumed it had something to do with my passing out," she said.

"Just a thought," Derec replied. "I'm trying everything on for size right now."

"Anyway," she continued, "he went off, against supervisory request, and turned up dead a short time later. When the utility robot tried to turn the body over to take a pulse, another room sealed itself off, and the robot just barely survived the sealing because of his quick reflexes. That's it. The whole story."

He leaned against the curled lip of the disc on stiff arms, trying to reason the way a computer would. "You know," he said after a minute, "the phrase 'alien contamination' could cover a lot of territory. On surface, human beings and their composition are obvious. But, under the surface, on the body's interior, we're all quite a strange collection of 'alien' germs and viruses."

"The bleeding foot," Katherine said. "That thought occurred to me, but I was never able to connect it with the actual murder, so I assumed it to be inconsequential."

"Me too," Derec replied. "But I'm beginning to think that, perhaps, this puzzle works on more than the obvious level." He knelt on the ground, studying the cut-out piece of city-robot that lay on the disc surface.

"What are you doing?" Katherine asked.

"This piece has been taken off stream," he said. "It's not connected to the city anymore, or to its programming source."

"So?"

"So it's dead, it's the only thing around here that isn't going to protect me from its jagged edges."

"You're going to hurt yourself!" she said loudly.

"There's only one way to test our theory," he said, rolling up the sleeve of his one-piece.

Rec poked his head out of the room. "Please, Friend Derec, don't do anything that could cause harm to your body."

Derec ignored both Katherine and Rec, drawing his forearm across a sharp edge of the dead city part, making a five-centimeter gash along his inner arm.

He stood, grimacing with the pain, then watched the dark blood well up from the place.

"Nothing yet," Katherine said.

"Let's try an experiment," Derec said, turning his arm over so the blood could drip on the disc. "The second sealed room didn't develop until the utility robot rolled the body over. Maybe gravity. . ."

"Derec!" Katherine yelled.

No sooner had the blood hit the floor than the curled lip of the disc began growing, pushing in and up, trying to close them in.

"Let's get out of here!" Derec called, moving toward the stairs, the disc curling up over his head like a cresting wave as he moved.

With Katherine right behind, he reached the stairs leading down, only to have them disappear before he could plant a foot on them. Overhead, the roof of the already existing room was stretching itself out, joining the edge of the disc in a perfect, seamless weld. Where the stairs had been was now a solid wall.

"Keep moving around the disc!" Derec called, breaking into a trot. "Maybe we can beat the enclosure."

He had turned his arm back over now, trying to catch dripping blood on his free hand to keep it off the ground. But it didn't help. The city-robot had isolated him as the alien carrier and was reacting to *him* now, and not his blood.

They went around the perimeter of the room, the roof hurrying to meet the curling disc. It had closed them in completely.

Then, as they watched, the already existing room seemed to melt and combine with the floor, the outer walls straightening and angling to ninety degrees, then pushing in all around.

Within a minute, they found themselves standing in a sealed room, exactly like the one David had been cut out of.

CHAPTER 11
DEADLY AIR

Derec and Katherine sat on the floor of the room, while Rec, who'd been trapped with them, leaned close to Derec, witnessing the boy wrapping his cut arm in a piece of cloth ripped from his one-piece.

"Do you think Eve's called for help?" he asked Rec as he worked.

"No," the witness said. "Eve will not perceive a danger to you. Are you in danger?"

"What about the utility robot?" Katherine asked, ignoring the robot's question. "Will the utility robot summon help?"

"That is within the scope of the utility robot's field prerogatives," Rec replied, straightening as Derec finished. He then wheeled slowly around the room, taking everything in for later recounting. Rec took his job very seriously.

Derec had left two loose ends on the tight bandage, and held his arm out to Katherine to tie them. "Can I trust you to tie a good knot?" he asked.

"What's that supposed to mean?" she asked.

"Nothing," he said.

She frowned deeply as she tied. "What happened in that office?" she asked. "You've treated me like your worst enemy ever since you came out of there." She pulled the knot tight, a smile touching her lips when he groaned loudly.

"Look," he said. "You've got secrets, I've got secrets. Why don't we just leave it at that?"

"Fine with me," she said. "All I want is for us to get the

rest of this together; then I'll make an emergency hyperwave call and be out of your hair in less than a day. You can rot here for all I care."

"We'll both rot here," he said, wanting to hurt her.

She drew back. "What do you mean?"

"Nothing."

"Damn you!" she yelled. "Tell me what you mean? Why did you say I'd rot here?"

"No reason."

"It's the hyperwave, isn't it?" she asked. "They won't give us access to the hyperwave."

"It's not that, it's . . ."

"It's what? What?"

He leaned his head back and shut his eyes. "There is no hyperwave transmitter," he said softly.

She pulled herself a distance from him and curled into a small ball. "You're lying," she said, but he could tell that she really believed him.

"The robots have no contact with the outside," he said. "They have no spaceport for landing ships. They have no hyperwave, or even the equipment for making one. They've been evasive about the point because of the security alert."

"Why have you waited until now to tell me this?" she asked.

"I told you—you've got secrets, I've got secrets."

"I get it now," she said, her eyes distant. "We're both free agents, looking out for ourselves."

"Something like that," he said, but why did it hurt so bad to say it?

She stood and moved all the way across the room to sit on the wall opposite. "Well, I suppose, at this point, we must work together to solve the murder," she said.

"I suppose," he replied, sorry to have started the whole line of conversation.

Her face was hard. "After that, I will thank you to stay away from me. We'll each take care of our own problems."

"Fair enough."

"So tell me, if it's not a great secret, why the room sealed around us because you cut yourself?"

"I've got a theory, nothing more," he said. "The city-robot is programmed to protect human and robot inhabitants and to defend itself against anything alien . . . foreign to it. Apparently blood inside the body is fine, but once it gets outside the body, its natural microbes register as alien and set off the works. The city program has to be fairly complicated. The omission is obvious, and could either have been a mistake or a deliberate glitch to test the ability of the robots and humans living here to control their own system."

"What do we do now?"

"Well, once we get out, if I can get access to the central core with one of the supervisors, I can reprogram the core to accept human blood as a natural microbe on the body of the city. In this sterile atmosphere, it's perfectly understandable how such a glitch could happen. It could even be a means for the city to protect itself from infection."

"But how did David die?" Katherine asked.

"Could it have been blood loss?" Derec asked.

She shook her head. "No chance," she replied. "There was very little blood. The cut was smaller than yours."

"What's left?" he said. "I have to think that his death is a completely separate incident, unconnected to the blood loss."

She looked skeptical. "Back-to-back coincidences, Derec? Deadly coincidences at that."

He stood. "You're right, of course. It must all tie together . . . but how?" He paced the room. "What other leads do we have? The only other connection is the fact that both of you came away from a sealed room with a headache."

"We have another problem," she replied, watching him moving back and forth in the confined space. "When I came in this room the first time to find the body, it had been sealed up . . . air tight."

He stopped walking and stared at her. "The city would never keep us locked up without air. It would be a violation of the First Law, should we die."

"It happened to David."

"But David was already dead when it happened to him," Derec said. "In fact, this just strengthens my theory. When the utility robot rolled him over to check for signs of life, gravity pulled a little more blood out of an already open wound. The room didn't relate to David as a human, since he was dead. All it fixed its sights on was the 'infection.' We're still alive and the city-robot knows it. Whatever else this crazy place may be, it's run robotically. Ipso facto, we're safe on that account."

"Just the same," she said, "I'll be happier to be out of here."

"Me too."

"You realize, Derec," she said, her voice low and heavy with meaning, "that we are recreating history right now. We are going through exactly the same progression that David went through before he died."

"I know," Derec replied. "But what else can we do?"

They stared at one another across the space of the room, the witness recording it all, and they may as well have been a million kilometers apart. They sat that way for a long time, far longer than it should have taken for a supervisor to show up.

Derec spent the time alternately trying to think his way out of their dilemma, figure out what was going on with Katherine, and looking at his watch. And the late morning turned to early afternoon, and Derec, who wasn't worried about the air supply in the room, suddenly became very thirsty and began to dwell on the possibility that the robots had either forgotten them or couldn't find them.

"Friend Derec!" came a loud voice from outside the room. "Friend Katherine! It is I, Wohler, the philosopher!"

Derec glanced at his watch. It was nearly five P.M., which

meant rain was undoubtedly on the way. "We're in here!" Derec called. "Can you get us free?"

Wohler called back loudly, "An Auroran philosopher once said, 'Freedom is a condition of mind, and the best way to secure it is to breed it.' Ho, Derec. We were held up digging in the mines, but I now have a laser torch to cut you out. I am here on the west wall of this room. I will ask kindly that you move to the east wall to avoid the torch as well as possible!"

Derec was sitting against the west wall. He stood immediately and moved over near Katherine, who looked at him with unreadable eyes.

"Go ahead!" Derec yelled through cupped hands, Rec moving up closer to the west wall to witness the torching from the inside.

Even through the thickness of the wall, they could hear the hiss of the torch on the other side. Derec slid down the wall to sit next to Katherine. Their arms accidentally touched. Both of them pulled away.

"Something's wrong," she said. "Something feels wrong."

"I know," he replied, "but what?"

The inside of the wall began to glow red hot in a small, circular section. Then the red turned to white, and a rivet-sized section burned through to reveal the outside through a quivering haze of heat.

Derec watched the hole expand, his mind racing as the torch began to etch the beginnings of a human-sized circle in the side of the room. He thought about headaches, and about erratic behavior and about blood and its composition—and then he thought about the nature of the city-robot.

"Stop!" he yelled, jumping to his feet and running as close to the metal cutting as he dared. "Stop the torch!"

"Derec?" Katherine asked, beginning to stand.

Derec covered his mouth with his hand. "Get on the floor!" he yelled. "All the way down and cover your mouth!"

"What's wrong?" came Wohler's voice from outside, the sound of the laser winding down to nothing. "What is it?"

"We can't use the torch on the wall!" Derec called.

"I don't understand," Wohler said, bending down so that his eye covered the hole in the wall and he could look inside.

Derec backed away, getting down close to Katherine on the floor. "Is there some way to flush oxygen in here?" he asked loudly.

"We've come in a newly manufactured emergency truck," Wohler replied. "I believe the emergency equipment includes oxygen cylinders."

"Get one quickly!"

"The rains are approaching," Wohler said. "We must hurry and get you out."

"Listen," Derec said. "The city material is a kind of metallic skin, an iron/plastic alloy. In the manufacturing process, a great deal of carbon monoxide is used as the reducing agent. I think your torch is liberating the monoxide as a gas into the closed room. By cutting us out, you're gassing us!"

"The utility robot has gone for the oxygen!" Wohler said. "You have my apologies."

"You didn't know," Derec said. He looked at Katherine. "Are you all right?"

"So far," she replied. "Are you sure of what you're saying? David didn't die until later, outside of the room."

"It doesn't matter," he replied. "Carbon monoxide in large doses will simply work its way gradually through the bloodstream, bonding firmly with hemoglobin and starving the tissues of oxygen. His headache and erratic behavior were the first signs of an oxygen narcosis reaction and, unless he was treated to massive doses of oxygen, it would spread throughout his entire body, eventually killing him."

"And *my* headache?"

"You walked into the room with his body just after they had cut through the walls," he said. "You undoubtedly saved your own life by passing out when you did, for they took you out of the room immediately, thus limiting your exposure to the gas. Carbon monoxide is colorless, odorless, and tasteless. You would never have known what hit you."

"The oxygen is here, Derec!" Wohler called, fitting a hissing nozzle up against the hole.

Derec crawled across the floor toward the hole. "Come on," he said, waving her on.

They reached the hole and sat breathing the life-giving oxygen. Derec felt the beginnings of a small headache, but he was sure it would get no worse.

They emptied the cannister of oxygen and began another. When that was finished, Wohler returned to the opening. "Rain is imminent," the robot said. "How do we get you out? We have nothing small to cut through this, and our heavy equipment can't be brought up this high, at least not with the rain coming. Do we leave you for the night?"

"There's no time for that," Derec said. "I must get underground and report this information to the central core."

"The rain is also dangerous for me, Friend Derec," Wohler said. "I must take shelter soon."

"Okay," Derec said. "Stay with me as long as you can. Just let me think for a minute."

"Derec . . ." Katherine began.

"Shhh," Derec said. "Not now."

"Think about your arm," she said. "Think about where you cut it, and how."

"My arm, I . . ." He held his arm up, looking at the blood-soaked bandage and feeling the throb. "I cut it on the dead piece of city-robot," he said.

"Because . . ."

"Because it was the only piece of the city that would *allow* me to cut myself on it!" He put his hands to his head. "That's it! Wohler! Stand back. We're coming through."

With that, he raised his right hand, pushing his pointer

finger through the small, burned-out hole. As soon as his finger grazed the jagged edge of the hole, it expanded to allow free passage. Next came his balled-up fist; the hole expanded wide to keep from cutting him. Then his arm went through, followed by head and shoulders. Seconds later, he was standing on the disc, its edges curling up to protect him. Katherine followed him through, and both of them stared into the teeth of a bitter cold wind and a savage vision of blue-purple clouds crackling with lightning.

"We must go now!" Wohler said, his shiny gold body reflecting lightning flashes.

Suddenly, Katherine broke from the group, hurrying to the stairs.

"What are you doing?" Derec called to her, but she ignored him, charging as quickly as she could down the stairs.

"Perhaps she's hurrying to safety," Wohler said, as Rec made it through the hole in the wall.

"Perhaps," Derec said, but as he ran the rest of the disc and began to take the stairs, Katherine had already run to the tram that was still dutifully waiting. She barked some orders to the utility driver, and the unit sped off into the darkening night.

"What is happening?" Wohler called as he followed Derec down the stairs.

"I'm afraid something crazy," the boy answered, remembering a conversation they had had while waiting to be rescued.

They moved to the emergency van that Wohler had brought. "We must get you back to your apartment before the rain comes," the robot said.

"No!" Derec said. "Get me underground. I'll wait out the storm there. Then you've got to go after Katherine. I'm afraid of what she's doing."

A long streak of lightning struck the top of the pedestal right beside them, the metal clanging loudly and smoking.

"But where could she have gone, Friend Derec?" Wohler

asked as they all climbed aboard the large, white van.

"The Compass Tower," Derec said, voice heavy with dread. "I'm afraid she's climbing the Compass Tower."

The Quadrant #4 Extruder Station was less than ten minutes from the sealed room, with Wohler moving the emergency van along at the top speed possible that still allowed a safety margin for his passengers.

Derec watched the city speed past, its full-blown dance of thoughtless progress still continuing despite the gathering darkness, despite the fact that its course was suicidal. He feared for the city; he feared for Katherine, or whatever her name was. She was going for the Key, he was certain of that, trying to take herself out of the situation in the only way she knew how. He didn't expect that the Key would do her much good, but he could hardly blame her for trying. What frightened him was the danger she was exposing herself to by trying for the Key in the rain. He would have gone after her alone, but, having experienced the destructive power of Robot City's weather, he knew he'd be no help at all in a storm. Only a robot would have a chance.

Wohler jerked them to a stop before the Extruder Station entrance, a series of low, wide buildings constructing themselves from ground level. There was no robotic activity here now, no unloading of trucks. All had taken shelter from the impending storm.

"You think she's gone to the Compass Tower?" Wohler asked.

"I'm sure of it."

"She may have time before the storm to get inside to safety."

Derec looked at him, then reached out and put a hand on his shiny gold arm. "She's not going inside," he said. "She'll be trying to climb the pyramid."

"But why?"

"We hid something there, something she's trying to retrieve."

"I must go," Wohler said without hesitation. "She'll be killed."

"What will the rain do to you?" Derec asked as he climbed out of the van.

"Rain in ordinary amounts won't do anything," the robot replied. "City rain could force its way through my plating in a thousand different places and make its way into my electrical system. The limits of the damage at that point are a matter of imaginative speculation."

"I don't know what to tell you," Derec said. "If you don't go . . ."

"Katherine will die," the robot finished. "You can tell me nothing. My duty is self-evident. Good-bye, Derec."

Wohler looked back once to make sure the witnesses were off the van, then hurried off at a pace that didn't include the safety margin he had preserved with Derec in the cab.

"Come with me," Derec told the witnesses, and moved toward the now-closed entrance to the underground. Despite his fears for Katherine's safety, he had things to do. With his explanation of the murder and its connection to the city defenses, backed up totally by Rec's witness testimony, there was no doubt that he'd at least be able to get into the core and stop the replication. That wouldn't stop tonight's rain, however, or even future rains for a time; but it was a start.

He opened the outside door, then hurried inside, going down the stairs to the now-deserted holding area and its bank of elevators. This wasn't the same Extruder Station he'd been in previously, but it was set up exactly the same.

He walked quickly to the same elevator he had taken with Avernus when he'd gone underground. He got inside with the witnesses and pushed the down arrow. The lift began its long journey to the caverns below.

The elevator opened into the bustling cavern where the work of building Robot City continued unabated. There wasn't a supervisor in sight, however. There seemed to be activity at one of the darkened, unused mine tunnels at the west end of the cavern.

He began to move into the flow, then stopped, steeling himself. Deliberation, Avernus had said. As he stood on the edge of the activity, a long tram sped past him at a hundred kilometers an hour, passing within a few centimeters, his hair being pulled by its suction.

Deliberation. It was the only way.

"Stay with me," he told the witnesses. Then he set his body in line with his goal and shut his eyes, taking a blind step right into the fray.

He walked quickly, without hesitation, trying to direct his mind away from the feel of unrushing robots and vehicles that barely brushed him as they hurried past. Occasionally, he would open his eyes a touch, just to make sure he was still heading in the right direction. Then he'd squeeze them closed again, and keep walking.

He kept this up for nearly ten minutes as he crossed the great chamber without mishap. As he reached the safety of the mine entrance, he released a huge sigh that made him feel as if he'd been holding his breath the whole time.

A utility robot was stationed near the mine entrance, using an overhead pulley system to remove the spent batteries from a fleet of mine.trams and replacing them with charged batteries. The trams were parked three deep all around him.

"Robot!" Derec called across the cars to him. "Where can I find Supervisor Avernus?"

The utility robot pointed down the tunnel. "They are releasing some of the reservoir water into the abandoned tunnels. It may be dangerous for humans."

"Thanks," Derec said, then pointed to a tram. "Has this one been recharged?"

"Yes," the robot answered.

"Thanks again," Derec said, and climbed behind the steering mechanism. "Rec, Eve, get in."

As the robots climbed into the back of the tram, the utility called to Derec.

"Did you not hear me? It may be dangerous for humans in there."

"Thanks," Derec said again, waving, then keyed on the electric hum and geared the car down the dark tunnel.

As he sped down the tunnels, marking distance by counting the small, red lights spaced along the length, he passed other trams full of robots going the other way. They were uniformly dirty from digging, many of them dangling shorted-out appendages. Even for robots, they appeared grim. One tram they passed carried a robot shorting from the head, sparks arcing from his photocells and speaker.

He drove for several kilometers, climbing gently upward with the tunnel. Finally, he approached a large egg of light that threw long shadows against the rough-hewn walls. When he reached the place, he found a large number of utility robots, plus six of the seven supervisors, gathered around a drop-off in the tunnel.

He jumped from the tram and pushed his way through the crowd to approach the drop-off. It was the same area in which the robots had been digging the day before, only approached from the other side. A subsidiary tunnel, going upward, had been dug by hand, and it met the existing tunnel, which had been trenched out to carry water. The trench was empty. Euler and Rydberg were leaning out over the trench, looking up the newly dug tunnel, while Avernus sorted out those robots damaged beyond usefulness here, and sent them back down the tunnel.

Derec moved up to Euler. "I've solved the murder," he told the supervisor without preamble.

Both Rydberg and Euler turned to look at him. "What was the cause?" Rydberg asked.

"Carbon monoxide poisoning," Derec said. "When they tried to torch David out of the sealed room, carbon monoxide was released by the heating process into the enclosed space."

"It was our fault, then," Euler said.

"It was an unfortunate accident," Derec replied. "And I have witnesses." Both Eve and Rec hurried to join him.

"Two minutes," Dante called. The small robot was fiddling with a terminal hooked up in the back of a tram, his long digits moving with incredible speed over the keyboard.

"Two minutes until what?" Derec asked.

"Until the charge we placed by the reservoir wall brings the water down," Euler replied.

"I also know why the city is on security alert," Derec said. "It was because of David's blood. When he cut himself, the blood that dropped on the city-robot was mistaken for an alien presence because of the blood organisms. My witnesses will also corroborate that fact."

Euler spoke up. "Then we need to feed this information to the central core and stop the replication, if there's time."

"What do you mean, if there's time?" Derec asked.

Avernus joined the group. "We found a cavern that would hold all the water in the reservoir, thanks to your sonogram. Unfortunately, it will take a great deal of digging to reach it." Avernus pointed to the trench. "This diversion will do no more than put off the inevitable for one more day; then, instead of overflowing above, the water will overflow below, here in the tunnels."

"Where is the central core?" Derec asked. "If we can get to it and stop the replication, then we can use the digging machines to turn the trick before the next day's rain."

Avernus turned to Dante, looking at him over the heads of all the other robots. "Where is the core now?" he called loudly.

The little robot's digits flew over the keys while Euler spoke. "Even with the machines, we'd have to start digging almost immediately to reach the cavern in time."

"The core is in Tunnel J-33 at the moment," Dante called, "moving south by southwest at ten kilometers per hour." He hesitated briefly, then added, "Twenty centads."

Avernus turned abruptly from them all. "That is . . . too bad," he said.

"What do you mean, too bad?" Derec asked.

All at once, there was a rumble that shook the tunnel, dust and loose pebbles falling atop them. Derec nearly lost his footing on the quaking ground. Within seconds, a low roar filled the mines, growing in intensity with each passing second.

"It is too bad," Euler said loudly above the roar, "because the central core is in Tunnel J-33, on the wrong side of the trench, and the rains are beginning outside."

With that, tons of water came rushing down the new tunnel, slamming in fury into the trench below, churning, forthy white, dangerous and untamed. Derec watched in horrified fascination as his only possible route to the central core disappeared under a raging river that hadn't been there a second before.

Katherine's mind was as dark as the clouds overhead as her tram hurried through the streets of Robot City in the direction of the Compass Tower.

"I fear we won't make the Tower before the rains come," the utility driver told her. "We must take shelter."

"No," she said, determined that she'd keep them from taking away her last ounce of free will. "Go on. Hurry!"

"It is not safe for you out here," the robot insisted. "I cannot in all conscience take you any farther."

Katherine began to respond with anger, but feared it would arouse the robot's suspicions. "All right," she said. "Pull over at the next building."

"Very good," the robot replied, and brought the tram to an immediate stop before a tall building that had the words MUSEUM OF ART embossed in metal above the doors.

The robot got out of the tram and took Katherine by the arm to guide her. "This way, please," he said, and Katherine began to think the robots had been having meetings about human duplicity.

She allowed the robot to lead her into the confines of the building. "This is Supervisor Arion's project," he said, "to please our human inhabitants."

She looked around, taking note that the robot had used the word *inhabitant* instead of visitors. It merely confirmed what she already knew to be the case. They weren't going to let her go. They had no intention of letting her go. The robots needed someone to serve, and they'd keep the masters as slaves just to see that it came to be.

The first floor of the museum was full of geometric sculptures, many of them made from city material that moved through its own sequences, constantly changing shapes in an infinite variety of patterns.

After a moment, she asked, "Please, is it possible to contact Derec and tell him where we are? I'm afraid he'll worry."

"There should be a terminal in the curator's office," the robot replied. "Would you like me to do it for you?"

"Yes, please. I would be most grateful."

The robot hurried off immediately. As soon as he was out of sight at the far end of the building, Katherine turned and ran.

She got quickly out the front doors and down the short walk to the tram, taking the driver's position. It started up easily, and she was off. She had no idea of which streets to take to get to the pyramid, but its size made it a beacon. She simply kept moving toward it.

She concentrated on planning as she drove. The rain was very close now, and she didn't want to get caught in it, but it was worth the try to get out of the city. Derec had said there was a trap door from the office to the platform atop the structure. She'd go through the inside of the pyramid, then, to reach the top. The Key was hidden partway down the outside of the structure, and it would be far easier and faster to climb down from the top than to climb up.

The sky rumbled loudly as she drove; the wind whipped her long hair around her face. She was cold, but put it out of her mind as she concentrated on her objective. Why did he have to do it to her? Why did he have to go over to the other side? The city had become Derec's obsession. He apparently couldn't understand that she had to have freedom, that she couldn't live within its structure forever.

The pyramid loomed large before her. It lit up brightly as a bolt of lightning ran down its face. She skidded to a stop before it and jumped out of the tram, hearing a noise behind her.

There, two blocks distant, the robot that called itself Wohler was hurrying to intercept her. She turned and ran up to the entry. The city material melted away at her approach to allow her inside.

Once inside, she had no idea of where she was going. The only thing she remembered for sure was that she needed to keep going up. She ran the maze-like halls, taking every opportunity to climb stairs or take an elevator that would put her higher. About halfway up the structure, she heard an announcement over unseen loudspeakers that called attention to her flight and gave instructions for her apprehension.

At that, she doubled her pace, going full out. Her only hope of escaping was to reach the safety of the off-limits zone before she was spotted.

She hurried unseen down the now-shortened hallways, reaching the last elevator up. A tech robot with welder arms spotted her as she hurried inside. Heart pounding, she stabbed at the up arrow and the machine sped her quickly to the upper floor.

The doors slid open and she burst through, running immediately. There were voices behind, calling her by name. She turned a corner, ran up a short ramp, and burst into the off-limits hallway just as the robots behind were closing on her.

She ran to the door leading up to the office, her hand going to the power stud.

"Katherine."

She recognized Wohler's voice and turned to face him. He stood, a hallway full of robots behind him, at the edge of the off-limits zone, the same place the witnesses had stopped earlier in the day.

"What do you want?" she asked.

"Come away from there. This place is off-limits."

She smiled. "Not to me," she said. "I'm human, remember? I'm free, and I'm going to be freer."

"Please do not go outside," Wohler said. "The rains are beginning. It could be dangerous for you."

"You're not going to keep me here," she said, opening the door that faced the spiral staircase.

"We would love to have you stay with us," the robot said, "but we would never keep you here against your will."

"Then why don't you have the means on-planet for me to leave or call for help?"

"You act as if we brought you here under false pretenses," Wohler said. "We did nothing. You came here uninvited. Welcome . . . but uninvited. Our civilization has not developed to the point where planetary interaction is possible. You can see that for yourself."

"We're wasting time," Katherine said, and started through the door.

"Please reconsider," the robot called. "Don't put yourself in jeopardy."

She stared hard at him. "I've been in jeopardy every second I've been in this crazy place."

With that, she moved through the door, closing it behind her. She took the stairs quickly and entered the office. The angry clouds rolled up close to the viewers, making it seem as if she were standing in the midst of the gathering storm.

Searching the office, she found the ladder easily enough, climbing it to reach the windy platform above. The wind was so strong that she feared getting to her feet, and crawled to the edge where she and Derec had made their first treacherous descent into the city of robots.

For the first time since being freed from the sealed room, her fears began to overcome her anger at the situation as she turned her body to edge herself off the dizzying height to begin her climb downward. The wind pulled viciously at her like cold, prying hands; her ears and nose went numb, and her fingers tingled with the cold.

Though the pyramid was made from the same material as the rest of the city, it wasn't the same in any other respect. It was rigid and unbending, its face set with patterns of holes that she and Derec had used as hand and footholds previously, and in which they had hidden the Key on their first descent.

Her mind whirled as she climbed, slowly, so slowly. How far down had it been? She had been moving fast, and Derec, carrying the Key, had been unable to keep up. They had stopped for a conference and decided to hide the Key and continue without it. How far down? A fourth of the climb, barely a fourth, in the leftmost hole of the pattern that ran down the center of the structure.

She continued downward, her fingers hurting now, her eyes looking upward, trying to gauge her distance just right. She began testing the holes in the repeated pattern, to no avail. She still hadn't reached the place. Something wet and cold hit her hard on the back. Her hands almost pulled out of their holds reflexively. It was a raindrop, and it wet the entire back of her one-piece.

She was running out of time.

The pattern of holes repeated again as she inched downward, and when she looked up, squinting against the frigid wind, she *knew* she had reached the place.

Hugging the pyramid face with the last of her strength, she slowly reached out, sticking her hand into the leftmost hole of the pattern.

The Key was gone.

"No!" she screamed loudly into the teeth of the monster, and, as if in response, the rain tore from the heavens in blinding, bludgeoning sheets to silence her protests.

* * *

Derec stood at the exit door to the Extruder Station and listened to the rain pounding against the door, and watched the small puddle that had somehow made its way under the sealed entry. Katherine was out there somewhere, and Wohler. Nothing had been heard from either of them since before the start of the rain. Avernus had made contact with the Compass Tower, and though both had been seen there, neither was there now.

With the rain controlling the day, everything had come to a standstill, making searching impossible, making contact with the central core impossible, making everything except the almighty building project slow to nothing. It was maddening.

He pounded the door, his fist sinking in, cushioning. He wanted to open those doors and run into the city and find her for himself—but he knew what that meant. Most likely, nothing would be known until the rain abated the next morning.

He turned from the door and walked down the stairs to the holding area and the six robot supervisors who awaited him there. His mind was awash in anxiety.

"Supervisor Rydberg has proposed a plan, Friend Derec," Euler said. "Perhaps you will comment on it."

Derec looked at Rydberg, trying to bring his mind back to the present. Why did the woman affect him this way? "Let's hear your plan," he said.

"We can go ahead and devise our evacuation schedule for the robots working underground," Rydberg said. "It seems that when morning comes, you will be able to contact the core and halt the replication. It will be too late to dig through to the cavern in time, but at least we will have the opportunity to spare our mine workers before the floods."

"Why do you have to give up like this?" Derec said, exasperated. "You've heard the reasons for the defenses. Can't you just stop them now and use the digging equipment to begin excavating the cavern?"

Waldeyer, the squat, wheeled supervisor, said, "The central core is our master program. We cannot abandon it. Only the central core can judge the veracity of your statements and make the final decision."

"I'm going to reprogram the central core," Derec answered, too loudly. "I'm going to change its definition of 'veracity.' And besides, the Laws of Robotics are your master program, and the Second Law states that you will obey a human command unless it violates the First Law. I'm *commanding* you to halt the mining processes and begin digging through to the drainage cavern."

"The defensive procedures were designed by the central core to protect the city, which is designed to protect human life," Waldeyer replied. "The central core *must* be the determining factor in any decision to abandon the defenses. Though your arguments sound humane, they may, ultimately, be in violation of the First Law; for if the central core determines that your conclusions are erroneous, then shutting down the defenses could be the most dangerous of all possible decisions."

Derec felt as if he were on a treadmill. All argument ultimately led back to the central core. And though he was sure that the central core would back off once he programmed the information about human blood into it, he had no way to prove that to the robots who, in turn, refused to do anything to halt the city's replication until they'd received that confirmation from central.

Then an idea struck him, an idea that was so revisionist in its approach that he was frightened at first even to think out its effects on the robots. What he had in mind would either liberate their thinking or send them into a contradictory mental freeze-up that could destroy them.

"What do you think of Rydberg's plan?" Avernus asked him. "It will save a great many robots."

Avernus—that was it—Avernus the humanitarian. Derec knew that his idea would destroy the other robots, but Avernus, he was different. Avernus leaned toward the humane, a leaning that could just possibly save himself and the rest of Robot City.

"I will comment on the evacuation plan later," Derec said. "First, I'd like to speak with Avernus alone."

"We make decisions together," Euler said.

"Why?" Derec asked.

"We've always done it that way," Rydberg said.

"Not any more," Derec said, his voice hard. "Unless you can give me a sound, First Law reason why I shouldn't speak with Avernus alone, I will then assume you are violating the Laws yourselves."

Euler walked to the center of the room, then turned slowly to look at Avernus. "We've always done it this way," he said.

Avernus, the giant, moved stoically toward Euler, putting a larger pincer on the robot's shoulder. "It won't hurt anything, this once, if we go against our own traditions."

"But traditions are the hallmark of civilization," Euler said.

"Survival is also one of the hallmarks," Derec replied, looking up at Avernus. "Are you willing?"

"Yes," Avernus answered without hesitation. "We will speak alone."

Derec led Avernus to the elevators, then had a thought and returned to Euler. He unwrapped the fabric bandage from his cut arm and handed it to the supervisor. "Have the blood analyzed, the data broken down on disc so I can feed it to the core."

"Yes, Derec," Euler said, and it was the first time the supervisor had addressed him without the formal declaration, Friend. Maybe they were all growing up a little bit.

Derec then joined Avernus in the elevator, pushing the down arrow as the doors slid closed. They only traveled down for a moment before Derec pushed the emergency stop button; the machine jerked to a halt.

"What is this about?" Avernus asked.

"I want to make a deal with you," Derec said.

"What sort of deal?"

"The lives of your robots for one of your digging machines."

Avernus just stared at him. "I do not understand."

"Let's talk about the Third Law of Robotics," Derec said. "You are obligated by the Third Law to protect your own existence as long as it doesn't interfere with the First or Second Laws. In your case, with your special programming, I can easily extend the Third Law to include the robots under your control."

"Go on."

"My deal is a simple one. Rydberg has suggested an evacuation plan that could save the robots in the mines from the flooding that is sure to occur if the cavern is not excavated. That evacuation plan depends *completely* on my reprogramming the central core to halt the replication. For if I don't, the city will have to keep replicating, even to its own destruction . . . that destruction to include the robots who are working underground."

"I understand that," Avernus said.

"All right." Derec took a deep breath. What he was getting ready to propose would undoubtedly freeze out the positronics of any of the other robots; the contradictions were too great, the choices too impossible to make. But with Avernus . . . maybe, just maybe. "Unless you give me one of the digging machines so I can begin the excavation myself, I will refuse to reprogram the central core, thereby condemning all your robots to stay underground during the flooding."

Avernus red eyes flared brightly. "You would . . . kill so many?"

"I would save your city *and* your robots!" Derec yelled. "It's all or nothing. Give me the machine or suffer the consequences."

"You ask me to deny the central core program that protects the First Law."

"Yes," Derec said simply, his voice quieting. "You have *got* to make the creative leap to save your robots. Somewhere in that brain of yours, you've got to make a value judgment that goes beyond your programming."

Avernus just stood there, quaking slightly, and Derec felt tears welling up in his eyes, knowing the torture he was putting the supervisor through. If this failed, if he, in effect, killed Avernus by killing his mind, he'd never be able to forgive himself.

The big robot's eyes flashed on and off several times, and suddenly his body shuddered violently, then stopped. Derec heard a sob escape his own lips. Avernus bent to him.

"You will have your digging machine," the robot told him, "and me to help you use it."

CHAPTER 13
THE CENTRAL CORE

Even as Katherine clung doggedly to the face of the pyramid, she knew that her ability to hold on could be measured in no more than minutes, as the rain lashed savagely at her and the winds worked to rip her off the patterned facade.

The ground lay several hundred meters below, calling to her. As her body went totally numb in the freezing downpour, her strong survival instinct was the only thing keeping her hanging on.

Her brain whirled, rejecting its own death while trying desperately to prepare for it, and through it all, she could hear the wind calling her name, over and over.

"Katherine!"

Closer now, the sound grew more pronounced. It seemed to come from below.

"Katherine!"

For the first time since she'd begun her climb, she risked a look downward, in the direction of the sound. She blinked through the icy water that streamed down her face only to see an apparition, a gray mass moving quickly up the face below her, proof that her mind was already gone.

"Katherine, hang on! I'm coming!"

In disbelief, she watched the apparition coming closer. And as her arms ached, trying to talk her into letting go and experiencing peace, she saw a golden hand reach from under the gray lump and grasp a handhold in one of the cutouts.

Wohler!

"Please hold on!"

"I can't!" she called back, surprised to hear the hysteria in her own voice. And as if to reinforce the idea, her left hand lost its grip, her arm falling away from the building, the added pressure sending cramping pain through her right arm still lodged in the hole.

The robot below hurried his pace. The wind, getting beneath the tarp he wore to protect himself from the rain, pulled it away from his body to float like a huge, prehistoric bird.

"P-please . . ." she called weakly, her right arm ready to give out.

"Hold on! Please hold on!"

The urgency in his voice astounded her, giving her an extra ounce of courage, a few more seconds when seconds were everything. And as she felt her hand slip away for good and all, his large body had wedged in behind her, holding her up against the facade.

Wohler clamped solidly in hand and footholds just above and below hers and he completely enveloped her, protecting. She let herself relax, all the strength immediately oozing out of her, Wohler supporting her completely.

"Are you unhurt?" the robot asked in her ear.

"I-I think so," she answered in a small voice. "What happens now?"

"We can only wait," Wohler said, his voice sounding somehow ragged. "An old Earth proverb says, 'Patience is a bitter plant but it has sweet fruit.' Survival w-will be our fruit . . . Friend Katherine."

"Friend Wohler," she responded, tears mixing with the cold rain on her face. "I want to th-thank you for coming up here for me."

But Wohler didn't answer.

The supervisors as a group stood behind the gateway excavator that Derec and Avernus operated. Neither helping nor hindering, they simply took it all in, no doubt unable to appreciate the thought processes that had led the big robot to pull the machine away from his mining crews and their replication labors, to put it to work simply clearing a path for something that, at this point, was no more than mere potential.

Derec had seen excavators like these before. On the asteroid where he had first awakened to find he had no identity, the robots had used identical machines to cut out the guts of the asteroid in their search for the Key to Perihelion.

The gateway was a marvel, for it demolished and rebuilt at the same time. Derec sat with Avernus at the two cabin control panels, watching the boom arms cutting into rock face nearly a hundred feet distant. One of the boom arms bore rotary grinders, the other microwave lasers that tore frantically at the core of the planet, chewing it up as it went. There were numerous conveyors and pulleys for the removal and scanning of potential salvage material, but none of these were in use right now. They were simply grinding and compressing the excavated rock and earth, the gateway itself using the materials to build a strong tunnel behind—smooth rock walls, reinforcing synthemesh, even overhead lamps.

They were creeping toward the cavern, every meter a meter closer to possible salvation. They had been working through the night, Derec desperately trying to let the effort keep his mind off Katherine and Wohler. It wasn't working. There had been no word of them since before the storm had begun nearly ten hours ago. Had they been alive, he would have heard by now.

There was always the chance that Katherine had retrieved the Key and left, perhaps waiting out the rain in the gray void of Perihelion, or perhaps finding her way to another place. But that didn't explain Wohler's absence.

During the grueling hours spent working the gateway, Avernus and Derec had conversed very little, both, apparently, lost in their own thoughts. Derec worried for Avernus, who he knew was going through a great many internal recriminations that could only be resolved with a satisfactory outcome and subsequent vindication of his actions.

"Derec!" came Euler's voice from the newly built tunnel behind; it was the first time the robot had spoken to them since the operation had begun.

Derec looked at his watch. It was nearly five A.M. He shared a glance with Avernus. "Yes!" he called back.

"The rain has abated," Euler returned. "The missing have been located!"

Derec resisted the urge to jump from the controls and charge out of there. He still had work to do. He looked at Avernus. "What now?"

"Now we will see," the robot said. "We must locate the core and reprogram."

"Should I leave you here to continue operations and go with someone else to the core?"

"No," Avernus said with authority. "I am supervisor of the underground and know my way around it. I also . . . must know the outcome. Can you understand that?"

Derec reached out and punched off the control board, stopping new digging and bringing all operants to the standby position. "You bet I can understand it. Let's go!"

They moved out of the gateway, squeezing past stacked up cylinders to join the other supervisors in the tunnel behind. It was the first time Derec had looked back at their handiwork. The tunnel he and Avernus had made stretched several hundred yards behind them, nearly as far he could see.

"Where are Katherine and Wohler?" he asked. "Are they all right?"

"No one knows," Rydberg said. "They are clinging to the side of the Compass Tower, nearly a hundred meters above the surface, but they have not responded to voice communication, nor have they attempted to come down."

Derec's heart sank. They'd been out all night in the rain. It looked bad.

"Are rescue operations underway?" he asked.

"Utility robots are now scaling the Tower to determine the

extent of the problem for emergency disposition," Euler said.

"The central core," Avernus said to Dante. "Tell me where it is right now."

"Tell me honestly, Euler," Derec said. "Will my presence at the Tower facilitate the rescue operation?"

"Tower rescue has always been part of our basic program, for reasons no one can fathom," the robot said. "Standard operating procedure has already been initiated. You could only hinder the operation."

"Good," Derec said. Of course Tower rescue was standard. The overseer had worried that, should the trap door to the office below become jammed, he would be caught on the Tower, unable to get down. The almighty overseer didn't mind letting everyone else twist slowly in the wind, but he wasn't going to let himself be uncomfortable on the Tower.

Dante spoke up from the terminal in his tram car. "The central core is in Quadrant 2, Tunnel D-24, moving to the north."

Avernus nodded and looked at Derec. "We must hurry," he said, "lest all our work be in vain."

"Work is already in vain," Waldeyer said to Avernus. "Because of your unauthorized impoundment of the gateway excavator, the on-hand raw iron consignments have dropped dangerously low. Within an hour, replication efforts will begin falling behind schedule."

The big robot simply hung his head, looking at the floor.

"I pose a question to you all," Derec said. "If Avernus and I are able to get to the core and reprogram to halt the replication, will our work already done here enable us to dig the rest of the way through to the cavern before tonight's rain?"

"Barring work stoppage and machinery malfunction," Euler said, "we should just be able to make it. This, of course, is all hypothetical."

Derec just looked at them. There was no satisfaction to be gained from arguing at this point. It was time to deliver the goods. "Where's the data from my blood sample?" he asked.

Arion stepped forward and handed him a mini-disc. "Everything you asked for is in here," he said.

"Thanks," Derec said, taking the disc and putting it in his breast pocket. "Now, listen. We're going to the central core. As soon as we reprogram, we'll need you to begin work here again immediately so that no time is lost."

Arion took a step toward the gateweay. "It is now too late to move the excavator back to the iron mine and pick up our failed operation there, so I see no reason why the digging here shouldn't continue in your absence. There is no longer anything to lose. I will continue to work here, even as you approach the central core."

"No," Euler said. "Will *you* now violate your programming, and perhaps the Laws?"

"The program is already shattered," Arion said, moving into the innards of the gateway. "There is no putting it back together now."

Derec smiled broadly as he heard the standby board being brought to full ready by Arion. He walked over to Dante. "We'll need your tram," he said. "Now."

The fever had come on strong, and along with it, hallucinations. Katherine's world was a nightmare of water, a world of water always threatening to pull her downward, and through it all Derec/David, David/Derec, Derec/David, his face smiling evilly and becoming mechanical even as she watched, metamorphosing from human to robot and back again, over and over. He'd skim the cresting waves to take her in his arms, only to use those arms to pull her underwater—drowning her! Drowning!

"Katherine . . . Katherine. Wake up. Wake up."

Voices intruding in her world of water. She wanted them to go away, to leave her alone. The water was treacherous, but at least it was warm.

"Katherine . . ."

Something was shaking her, pulling her violently from her dream world. She opened her eyes to pain blazing like fire through her head.

It was daytime, early morning. A utility robot was staring at her around the protective branch of Wohler's arm.

"C-cold," she rasped, teeth chattering. "So . . . cold."

A light flared above her and to the left, a light raining sparks. She squinted. Welders were using laser torches to cut Wohler's pincers off the facade where they were locked tight. Above the welder, she could see mechanical pulleys magnetically clamped to the side of the structure, city-material ropes dangling.

"We are cutting you free," the robot said. "A net and stretcher have been strung just below you. You are safe now."

"C-cold," she rasped again.

"We will warm you. We will get you medical attention."

And through the haze that was her mind, she felt the reassuring firmness of Wohler's body protecting her, always protecting her.

"Wohler!" she said loudly. "We're s-safe. Wohler!"

"Supervisor Wohler is . . . nonoperational," the utility said.

Even through the hurt and the delirium, she was wracked by waves of shame. That this robot would give his life for hers, after the way she'd acted, was more than she could bear.

She felt his weight behind her give; then hands were lifting both of them onto the stretchers pulled up tight below. She felt the morning sun on her face, a sun that Wohler would never experience again, and rather than dwell on the unpleasant results of its own selfishness, her mind once more retreated into the blissful haze of unconsciousness.

"Would you have?" Avernus asked him as they pushed the tram down tunnel D-24, heading north.

"Would I have what?" Derec replied. The tunnel walls rushed past, red lights zipping overhead at two-second intervals.

"Would you have let the robots die if I hadn't agreed to help you dig the tunnel?"

"No," Derec said. "I wouldn't have done anything like that. I just wanted to talk some sense into you."

"You lied to me."

"I lied to save you," Derec said. "Remember our discussion about lying in the Compass Tower? I created a different reality, a hypothetical reality, to force you into a different line of thought."

"You lied to me."

"Yes."

"I do not know if I'll ever really understand that," Avernus said, subtly telling Derec that their relationship would forever be strained.

"I'll have to learn to live with that," Derec replied sadly. "Sometimes the right thing isn't always the best thing. I'm sorry if I hurt you."

"Hurt is not a term that I understand," the robot replied.

"No," Derec said, turning to fiddle with the terminal Dante had left in the back. "It's a term that I relate to."

Derec used the terminal to contact the city's hastily organized medical facility, trying for information on Katherine and Wohler. He and Avernus had left Quadrant #4 and traveled through the city to #2, going underground again at that point. Tunnel D-24 was one of the more distant shafts, drilled as an oil exploration point for the plastics operation. A pipeline churned loudly, attached to the tunnel ceiling above their heads.

"They've gotten Katherine and Wohler down from the Tower!" he said, wishing his fingers moved as well as Dante's over the keyboard.

"Are they well?"

"Katherine is suffering from shock and exposure," Derec

said excitedly. "She's being treated now. The prognosis is good. Wohler is . . . is . . ." He turned sadly to Avernus. "Wohler is dead."

"Look!" the robot called, pointing ahead.

Farther along the tunnel, they were rapidly closing on a moving area of light. It was perhaps six meters long, and just tall enough to miss the overhanging lights.

"The central core!" Avernus said, braking heavily, the tram skidding to a halt.

"What are you doing?" Derec asked. "It's getting away!"

"It will be faster now on foot," Avernus said.

"Not for me," Derec replied. "I can't run fast enough to . . ."

"Climb on my back," the robot ordered. "Quickly."

While the huge robot was still sitting, Derec stood and climbed onto his broad back, putting his hands around Avernus's head, the robot locking an arm behind him, holding Derec on tightly.

Then Avernus jumped from the cart and began a headlong charge down the tunnel, moving faster than Derec realized was possible. Tunnel segments flew by in a blur as the moving core grew larger and larger in their vision.

They caught it quickly, and Avernus slowed his pace to match the speed of the core. Its outer surface was transparent plastic of some kind, and very thick. Like a transparent eggshell, it contained the complex workings of a sophisticated, operating machine. In the rear was a platform with steps leading up to a sliding door.

Avernus jumped, catching the stairs and climbing on. He brought his arm around, gently lifting Derec off to stand before the door. "Go on," he said. "Go in. Only one at a time can pass through."

Derec slid open the door by hand and walked in to find himself within the transparent chamber. A red button was set in the plastic before him. He pushed it. Sprayers and heat lamps came on, a full body spray of compressed air traveling the length of his body to remove all traces of dust. There was a loud sound of suction, and then the wall before him slid open and he walked into the beating heart of Robot City.

The core was open, like an exposed brain, its working synapses sparking photons up and down its length, its fluidics a marvel of imaginative engineering. He found a typer halfway down its length and juiced it to life, while hearing Avernus going through the chamber ritual. The robot was doubled over to fit within the "clean room."

The first thing he did was open a file under the heading of HEMOGLOBIN, and enter the disc's-worth of information Arion had procured for him. Then he got into the DEFENSES file again, going as far as he could with the system until it prompted him for the supervisor's password.

He heard a door slide open and turned to see Avernus, still somewhat hunched over, move to stand beside him at the typer.

"It wants your password," Derec said.

Avernus looked at him, not speaking, then reached out and typed on the screen:

AVERNUS—2Q2-1719

PASSWORD: SYNNOETICS

Without a second's hesitation, the computer prompted:

RATIONALIZATION FOR DEACTIVATION OF CITY DEFENSES?

With shaking fingers, Derec typed his rationalization into the machine, dumping, as he did so, all the information from the HEMOGLOBIN file into the CITY DEFENSES file as authoritative backup and information to keep the same thing from ever happening again.

When he was through typing he stood back and took a breath, almost afraid to push the ENTER key.

"We must know now," Avernus said.

Derec nodded, swallowed hard, and entered the information.

The machine churned quietly for a moment that seemed to last an hour. Finally, quite simply and without fanfare, it responded.

RATIONALIZATION ACCEPTED—DEFENSES DEAC-
TIVATED.

They stood for a moment, staring, not quite believing that
it could be so easy. Then they felt a noticeable slowing of
the core's motion. Within seconds, it had ground to a stop.

It was over.

Derec walked the corridors of the mostly dark, mostly unfurnished medical facility. It would be a fine building when it was completely finished, a place where the humans who would inhabit Robot City could receive the finest medical care available anywhere in the galaxy under the supervision of the most advanced team of med-bots operational. He knew this would be so because the robots who performed the services would perform them by choice, out of love instead of servitude.

He walked the corridors alone—no guides, no keepers, no jailers. He was a free citizen now, a condemned man no longer. And it was good, because now, right now, he preferred being alone.

A room at the end of the corridor was awash with light, and he knew he'd find Katherine there, recovering from her night with the storm. He no longer cared about her subterfuge or her reasons for being with him on Robot City. For good or ill, he was happy and thankful that she was alive. Nothing else really could, or did, matter.

He was beginning to know why she affected him the way she did—he loved her.

He reached the room and poked his head inside. It was a large room, one that would most likely be a ward at some future time. But right now it was empty, except for Katherine's place at the far end.

She lay in stasis, floating half a meter above a table, bright lights surrounding her completely. She was naked, just as she'd been on Rockliffe Station. This time he didn't turn away, but looked, and her body seemed somehow . . . familiar to him.

A med-bot rolled up to him.

"How is she?" he asked.

"Splendid," the robot replied, "except for her chronic condition . . ."

"I don't want to talk about it," he said, letting her have her secrets. "Other than that?"

"She's sleeping lightly," the med-bot said. "We have re-balanced her chemicals through massive influxes of oxygen and fluids, and warmed her up. She lost a small part of her left ear to the cold, but that has already been adjusted through laser cosmetic surgery. You may visit with her if you wish."

"I'd like that," he said. "But before you wake her up, would you put a robe or something on her?"

"The heat lamps work better if . . ."

"I know," Derec said. "It's a matter of her personal privacy."

"I see," the robot said in its best bedside manner, but Derec could tell that it didn't.

When the med-bot turned and rolled back to Katherine, Derec politely stepped through the doorway and back into the hall.

A moment later, he could hear her talking to the robot, so he walked back in. She was off the table, sitting in a motorized chair, swathed in a bright white bathrobe. Her face was blank as he moved up to her.

"I'm sorry for everything," he said. "I've been suspicious and hard to get along with and . . ."

She smiled slightly, putting up a hand. "No more than I have," she said softly, her voice hoarse. "I guess I've acted pretty stupidly."

"Human prerogative," he said. "You look . . . good."

"They scraped the surface skin off me," she said, "cleared away the dead dermis. I guess I could say you're looking at the new me." She moved her gaze to the floor. "The Key is gone."

"I didn't know," he replied. "I guess we're really stuck."

She nodded. "Did you hear what . . . what Wohler did for me?"

"Yes."

"I never understood your . . . feeling for the robots," she said, eyes welling up with tears. "But his life was as important to him as mine is to me, and he . . . he gave it up . . . so I could live."

"He was burned out completely," Derec said. "They're trying to reconstruct him now."

She looked up at him. "Reconstruct?"

"It won't be the same, of course. We are, all of us, a product of our memories. The Wohler you knew is, for the most part, dead."

"But if they reconstruct," she said, "something of him will remain."

"Yes. Something."

"I want to go there," she said. "I want to go where he is."

She tried to stand, Derec gently pushing her back in the chair. "You're still a sick girl," he said. "You can't be running around doing . . ."

"No," she said, a spark of the old Katherine already coming back. "He died so that I could live. If there's anything of him left, I want to be there."

Derec drew a long breath. "I'll see what I can do," he said, knowing how stubborn she could be.

And so, thirty minutes later, Katherine, wrapped in a sterile suit, wheeled herself into the dust-free repair chamber where six different robots were working diligently on the body of Wohler, the philosopher. Derec walked with her.

Most of his plating was gone, circuit boards and relays hitting the floor with clockwork regularity, a small robot wheeling silently around and sweeping up the discards.

"Can I get closer?" she asked Derec.

"I don't see why not," he answered.

Just then, Euler came into the chamber and walked directly toward the couple. "Friend Derec," he said. Derec smiled at the reuse of the title before his name. "We are just completing work on the connecting tunnel to the runoff cavern and would very much like you to be present for the opening."

Derec looked down at Katherine. "Well, I'm kind of busy right now, I . . ."

"Nonsense," Katherine said, reaching out to pat his hand. "I'm just going to stay around here for a while. One of the robots here can get me back to medical."

He smiled broadly. "You sure it's okay?"

She nodded, smiling widely. "I understand completely," she said.

He grinned at Euler. "Let's go," he said, and the two of them moved quickly out of the room.

Katherine listened to their footsteps receding down the hall, then wheeled her chair closer to the work table. Her anger at Derec along with a great many other conflicting emotions, had died along with Wohler on the Compass Tower. Because of her thoughtlessness, a life had been lost. All her other emotions seemed petty in the face of that.

She wheeled up near the golden robot's head. Most of his body was exposed in pieces on the table, but the head and upper torso were intact. The robots working on the body moved around the table to accommodate her presence.

She stared at his head, reaching out a finger to gingerly touch him. "I'm so sorry," she said.

Suddenly, the head turned to her, its photocells glowing brightly. "Were you addressing me?" he asked her.

"Wohler," she said, jumping. "You're alive."

"Do we know one another?" he asked, and she realized that this was a different Wohler, a newly programmed Wohler who knew nothing of their previous experience.

"No," she said, choking back a sob. "My name is Katherine. I'm . . . pleased to make your acquaintance."

"A new friendship is like new wine," Wohler said. "When it has aged, you will drink it with pleasure. Katherine... Katherine. Why are you crying?"

Only a small dam held back the waters in the trench from the tunnel that Derec and Avernus had dug to the cavern. The supervisors and as many of the utility robots as could clusters in the opening were there, Derec holding the electronic detonator that would blast away the dam and open up the new waterway.

"This is the first day," Euler told him, "the first day in a truly unified city of humans and robots. The beginning of the perfect world."

"We have reacted synnoetically to make this day happen," Rydberg said. "Working together we can accomplish much."

"While we still have a great deal to learn about one another," Derec said, "I, too, believe that we have proven something of value here today."

"Then open the floodgate, Friend Derec," Euler said, "and make the connection complete."

"With pleasure."

Derec flipped the toggle on the hand control. A small explosion made the wall of dirt and rock jump. Then it crumbled, and rapidly flowing water from the trench finished the job that the explosive had begun.

And as the waters rushed past, he thought of all the things still unresolved, still rushing, like the waters, through his confused brain. Who was he? Who was the dead man? Who put this all together, and why?

And then there was Katherine.

In many ways, he still felt as if his journey had just begun, but he couldn't help but feel he had accomplished something major with the breaking down of the dam. He couldn't help but feel that something good, something positive had been accomplished. And that made him feel just fine. Maybe life was nothing so much as a succession of small battles, small victories to be won.

"Derec," came a voice behind him, and he turned to see Avernus standing there.

"Yes?"

The robot, so large, spoke with a small voice. "I do not know that I can understand why you did what you did to me last night," he said, "but I cannot help but feel that we did the right thing, and that doing the right thing is what is important."

"I couldn't agree more," Derec said, smiling widely. "Friends?"

Avernus nodded solidly. "Friends," he said, as he laid his pincer in Derec's open palm in the universal gesture of peace and good will.

It wasn't going to be such a bad day after all.

DATA BANK

Illustrations by Paul Rivoche

KATHERINE ARIEL BURGESS, "KATE": Kate is a native Auroran, banished from her homeworld because of an incurable disease. Despite her illness and a pampered upbringing, Kate is headstrong, tough, demanding, and resourceful. On the advice of the medical robot Galen, she refuses to tell Derec what she knows of his past life.

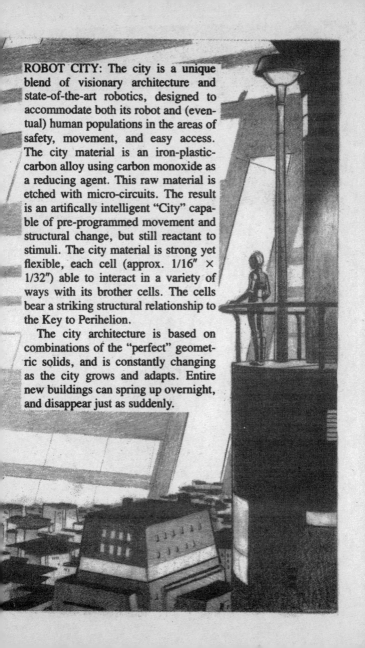

ROBOT CITY: The city is a unique blend of visionary architecture and state-of-the-art robotics, designed to accommodate both its robot and (eventual) human populations in the areas of safety, movement, and easy access. The city material is an iron-plastic-carbon alloy using carbon monoxide as a reducing agent. This raw material is etched with micro-circuits. The result is an artifically intelligent "City" capable of pre-programmed movement and structural change, but still reactant to stimuli. The city material is strong yet flexible, each cell (approx. 1/16″ × 1/32″) able to interact in a variety of ways with its brother cells. The cells bear a striking structural relationship to the Key to Perihelion.

The city architecture is based on combinations of the "perfect" geometric solids, and is constantly changing as the city grows and adapts. Entire new buildings can spring up overnight, and disappear just as suddenly.

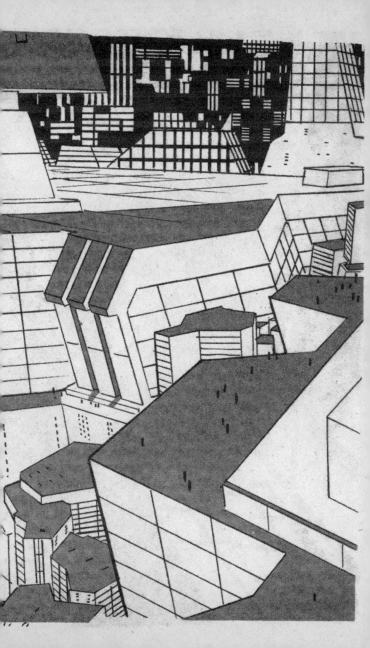

WITNESS ROBOTS: These robots contain specialized sensor equipment and are equipped to function only as event witnesses and reporters. Capable only of first-level (observation) connections, the witness robot has no lifting appendages, in order to maintain detached objectivity.

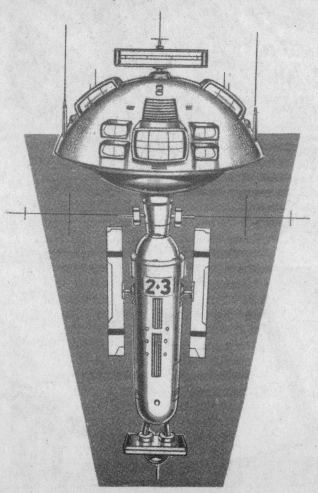

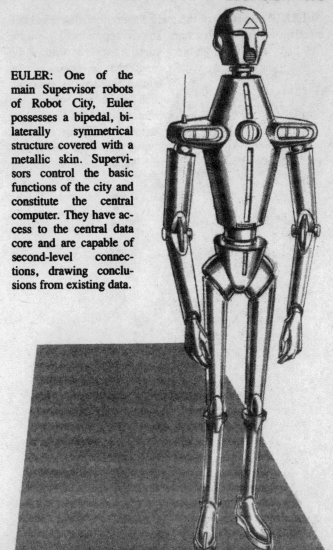

EULER: One of the main Supervisor robots of Robot City, Euler possesses a bipedal, bilaterally symmetrical structure covered with a metallic skin. Supervisors control the basic functions of the city and constitute the central computer. They have access to the central data core and are capable of second-level connections, drawing conclusions from existing data.

AVERNUS: Another of the main Supervisors, Avernus has a bipedal, humanoid structure, stands approximately twelve feet high, and has a jet-black metallic skin. Instead of the pseudo-hands possessed by human-oriented supervisors, such as Euler, Avernus has interchangeable hands for various functions. He is shown here with the human-oid hands he employs for very delicate work. His usual hands, however, are a set of highly adaptable pincer-like claws.

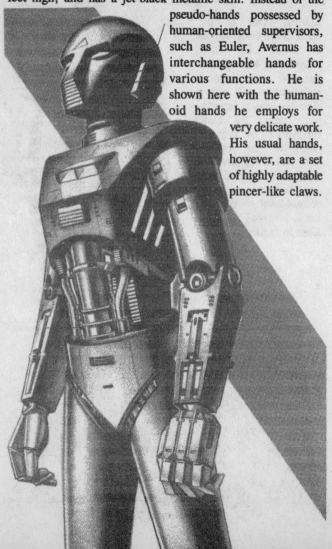

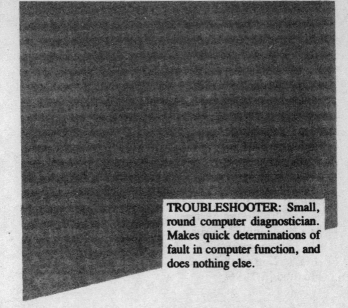

TROUBLESHOOTER: Small, round computer diagnostician. Makes quick determinations of fault in computer function, and does nothing else.

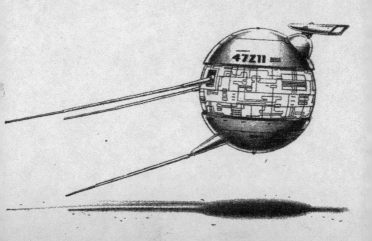

ABOUT THE AUTHOR

MIKE McQUAY began his writing career in 1975 while a production line worker at a factory. Before that, he worked a variety of jobs, including: musician, airplane mechanic, banker, retail store owner, bartender, Club Med salesman, and film pirate. Following the publication of his first novel, *Lifekeeper*, in 1980, McQuay published over 22 novels and short story collections in a variety of fields—science fiction, children's, horror, mainstream thriller, and adventure. He died in 1996.